1807

John Curry

We Run Bad

The Okie Doke Book Publishing Corporation
New York

ISBN 978-1-7324112-1-0

1

It's Tuesday night and there isn't much action, so Harris and I are going out to a club. In Atlantic City. In New Jersey. This is something I have never done before, and with reason.

Harris insists that I drive us to the Taj in *his* car, but he doesn't say why. I feel like something's up here, but I pretty much always feel that way around Harris, so I try not to be a little bitch about it and just take the keys and climb into the driver's seat. As we approach the parking lot gate, he pulls out a Black Card and hands it to me.

"Where the fuck did you get this?"

"I *obtained* it from a man named ... uh ... *Dejian Bui.*" Harris laughs and throws it in my lap.

"Jesus Christ, did you steal this from an Asian man?"

"Just give it to her, she's a fucking parking lot attendant, what the fuck does she know?"

This is standard Harris—a man I've seen dust off a

teacher's salary in a single weekend, and now he's risked jail time by stealing a man's comp card in an effort to waive the $5 parking fee at the casino gate. I reluctantly hand the Asian baller's Black Card to the lady in the booth. She looks at the card, then looks down into the vehicle and sees two white males in a shit-beaten Sonata, then asks us for ID. Harris leans over me and barks from the passenger side, "Our ID is on the fucking *card*! We don't have any other ID!"

Immediately, I interrupt the argument that's about to ensue and tell her that the card belongs to a friend of ours—that he was kind enough to let us use it for the weekend. She lies right back to us, says the card's expired, and that she's obligated to hold it until "Mr. Bui" comes back to claim it. So I pay the $5 and get us the fuck out of there before we're banned from the casino, or worse.

As we exit the parking lot, I look over at this ne'er-do-well beside me, and now I can see why he wanted me to drive us this evening. Right next to me, and as if it were the most natural thing in the world, the son of a bitch starts tying off. You know, like what a heroin user does.

"Drive slow," he tells me. "No sudden stops or turns. I can't afford to spill this shit right now."

I do as he says. If I tell him I'm uncomfortable with him shooting up while I'm driving (which I am), he'll most likely insist on taking the wheel himself while still attempting his routine. I've seen him do it before—steering with his knees, his hat turned backwards, looking up, looking down, looking up, looking down, making sure not to spill his precious *shit* as we idle from stoplight to stoplight.

I glance over at Harris and watch him out of the corner of my eye for a few seconds. There's something undeniably *alien* about this man—this 33-year-old white male in an Ed Hardy t-shirt trying to heat up five bags of heroin with the dashboard cigarette lighter of a Hyundai Sonata. This is also a man who burned his mother's house down with a lit joint when he was fourteen; a man who also, at nineteen years of age and high as fuck, robbed his first bank with a piece of paper that read "I have a BOOM." It was supposed to say "I have a BOMB," but he was too fucked up at the time to pull it off. Yes. This is a man, some would say, who has no future. And yet, every time I'm forced to share a room with him, he's over there sleeping like a goddamn baby—even on the nights after he's lost enough to feed villages.

Thinking about it all right now threads tension through my nerves as I watch this person beside me prepare hardcore drugs under the scrim of dark and slow, shady-as-fuck, late night cruising the streets of Atlantic City.

As we pull up to an intersection and stop at the light, I take a good look around at this place. I've never really noticed it before (because I almost never leave the casino), but this might be one of the worst cities in America. I've never seen so many 24-hour pawnshops and liquor stores—broke-down, half-lit marquis for Payday Loans, Instant Check Cashing, and We Buy Gold. Every human on the streets looks hazardous in some way. This is the kind of place where people vanish and no one notices, or no one gives a shit. The ocean's right there, ready to swallow up all the world's garbage.

I turn to look out my window and see an AC police cruiser creep up next to us. I look away casually, like there's not a man in possession of a Schedule I narcotic sitting right next to me, ready to slam it up his arm. I signal and turn down the next block and onto the boulevard. Thankfully, they don't follow.

After Harris finally gets his dope cooking, we're already at the garage. He finishes the rest of his routine rather quickly, then jams it in. It doesn't seem to faze him—like at all. He gets out of the car, bends down to check his hair in the passenger-side mirror, then, somewhat gingerly, places a toothpick between his teeth. And there you have it: a head full of dope, slick wet hair, and b-grade designer denim pockets stuffed to the tits with cash. *Made as fuck in America.*

When we get to the Casbah, there's this big, fat

Hispanic bouncer wearing an ill-fitted black suit and black leather gloves with the knuckles cut out. Suddenly, a nasty feeling zaps me in the guts. My autonomic nervous system screams at me to turn back around. *Get out! Run!* I feel like I need to get back to my hotel room immediately and lie down for a few minutes. But it's too late. We've come this far, and Harris is ready for action. The gravity of the evening is pulling us in. We have arrived, we are totally fucked, and now there is nothing we can do about it.

"Twenty bucks," demands the bouncer.

"But it's fuckin' *Monday,* bro," Harris whines at him.

"Today is Tuesday, kid, and it's twenty dollars."

"Ah come on, dude, this is *bullshit!* We came all the way down here from Long Island—isn't that right?" Harris looks back at me for affirmation.

"Yup, Long Island," I manage to repeat.

"Twenty bucks," the guy says, for what's clearly going to be the last time.

Harris looks down, shaking his head in defeat, takes the toothpick out of his mouth, turns his back to the bouncer, reaches in his pocket, wets his thumb with his bottom lip and peels off two twenties from his roll. Puts the toothpick back into the side of his mouth, then hands the guy the forty bucks and says, "Okay, but normally I would *never* do this." The guy rolls his eyes as he stamps us with some kind of mucousy invisible ink. He then opens the doors to let us in as I attempt to apologize for Harris's behavior, but my words are instantly blanketed by the terrible music that comes spilling out at us. I just stand there for a few seconds, sort of staring at the guy, bewildered, and then he pushes me along like some terrified kid who's about to have his first time on the big-boy ride. And it suddenly occurs to me, that in many passive but meaningful ways, I've been avoiding this moment my entire adult life.

When we walk inside, I notice immediately that the club is practically empty, save for some South Jersey types enjoying bottle service over at the VIP booth in the corner—looks like somebody's birthday maybe. They're drinking from a bottle of alcohol shaped like a human skull. It's resting inside a bucket of dry ice lit from the bottom by blue LEDs and there's about ten cans of Red Bull flanked up all around it just waiting to make everyone insane.

And this is what you can have in America on your birthday: alcohol served on ice that's *literally colder than fucking ice*, contained within a crystal effigy of human remains and complimented by mixers, that in certain quantities, are arguably more powerful and deadly than cocaine. *Now try and tell me we ain't fuckin' free in this country.*

The dudes all have a fuck-ton of product in their hair, and they wear pastel-colored polos with the collars popped up and hanging limp around their ears. Each of them has a thick, brightly colored silicone bracelet on each of their *left* wrists; I assume this is because wearing a brightly colored silicone bracelet on the *right* wrist means you're a fucking faggot.

Harris leans into the bar, almost sideways, his right elbow on the rail, hands folded, his mouth protruding out a little, as he scrutinizes the overweight cooze twerking and grinding on the dance floor. The only skinny girls here are the ones in the little VIP enclave, which gives me a bad feeling, because I'm pretty sure Harris is going to go for it. I doubt anyone over there will appreciate his advances.

I order a Jack and Coke at the bar. "Eighteen," says the bartender. He also has a brightly colored silicone bracelet on, and his arms are shaved and tanned. He hands me the drink, and I notice immediately there's hardly any Jack in my Coke as I walk to the other side of the bar to take a seat. I'll have to order a beer next. At least I'll know how much alcohol is in that.

Already I see Harris is in trouble. As I predicted, he went in for the kill, bare-assed, dick-waving, and screaming at the enemy. Completely unprepared. He probably started talking to the girls without even acknowledging the three dudes. The girls are still sitting there, but now all three dudes are standing around him in that triangular attack formation: one to his back and two at his flanks, their arms all crossed, their foreheads all scrunched up and pissed-off looking.

All doped and dolled up for this evening's affairs, Harris confidently persists with hitting on the hottest girl in their party. Then I see him turn to one of the dudes, say some shit with his hands (which looks undeniably offensive) and within seconds a pathetic little skirmish breaks out just as the strobe lights all go apeshit with the breakdown in the music. All I can really see now are the strobes flashing over flailing arms, pink polo fabric and wet, black hair spikes. Instead of jumping in and trying to save his ass, I try and slam the rest of my drink as fast as I can because I'm pretty sure we're both getting kicked out of this place, and I just paid $18 for this piece of shit.

"Are you alright?" Outside the club now, I'm standing over Harris as he's sticking a twisted-up tissue into his nose, examining the flow of blood.

"Yeah, I don't even give a fuck. I can barely feel it anyway. Fucking bullshit though. Twenty bucks at the door and the only fuckable girl there was that stuck up little Jersey slit with the $3000 purse. Pretty damn hot though. I think her name was *Alexis* or some shit. It's a shame she was such a stuck up little snooty hoot."

"Yeah, well, you give your daughter a name like *Alexis*, she's just going to grow up *wanting* shit."

"True that," Harris sighs. "Fuck it. You wanna chop

up a hooker with me?" I know what Harris means here; he doesn't literally mean *chop up a hooker*, like dismember her. A "chop" to a card player means a split pot. What Harris is saying to me right now is that he wants me to split the cost of a hooker with him. He asks me this with the same nonchalance you might ask a friend to split an appetizer with you.

"No," I tell him, plainly.

"Alright, well," he sighs, "I guess I'm just going to have to fuck her *twice as hard* then. I'll catch up with you later. I'm gonna go score some *birth canal*. Peace, bro."

All alone now, standing outside a dance club in The Taj Mahal—not the one in India, the one in Atlantic City, the one in fucking New Jersey—I decide to call it a night and take it easy for the remainder of the evening.

Technically, I have a room back across town that I'm supposed to be sharing with Harris tonight, but I decide instead to check into a room here, because God only knows what Harris is going to bring back there later when I'm trying to relax and find a few moments' peace. I could really use some alone time anyway.

I haven't been laid in over six months, and I've been sharing a hotel room with basically complete strangers, so resisting the Taj's "adult entertainment" selection isn't even an option right now.

After jacking off like a madman, I watch some regular TV but nothing's good, so I decide to get a little load on—just a touch to keep my mind entertained and help me fall asleep. The bar's too expensive for my liking, and I don't feel like playing slots right now, so I clean myself up and make for the nearest liquor store, which is only about three blocks from the casino.

I take the elevator down to the lobby, and on my way toward the exit I see several security personnel attempting to restrain a senior *citizen* from strangling one of the blackjack dealers. After a good thirty-second struggle, they finally chokehold the sloppy old bastard and pin him to the floor. He begins sobbing and apologizing, his voice muffled into the thick, plush, purple carpeting. "I don't *want* to go to jail! I just don't want to *lose* anymore! I'm Sa-ha-ha-RRY! I'm so *sorry*! Ahh Gawwwd!"

And this is one thing you should probably know about gaming culture in America. When you emerge from those brass elevator doors and you find yourself after midnight among the scrums of elderlies slamming decaf, chain smoking long thin cigarettes, and beating the fuck out of slot machines, even if you've yet to wager a single dollar in this place you need to understand *one thing*: just being here means you've already lost.

And now I'm on a quest to find a liquor store, so I can get drunk alone and cheaply in my casino hotel room, while I watch HBO and try to fall asleep before the suicide ideation kicks in.

Three city blocks in arguably one of the worst oceanfront towns in America, by virtue of some miracle, I make it into the "pharmacy" without incident or confrontation. It's not a pharmacy per se; it's more like a liquor store with condoms, Pepto-Bismol, lube, potato chips, and antacids. As I approach the bulletproof glass at the counter, I figure a pint of shitty gin ought to do the trick. *Yeah, gin. The reason British people don't need NyQuil.* Gin has an almost medicinal quality to it, and I could do with a good mind-erasing right now. I need the kind of hang-over that will make me not want to drink again for a good long while, and this $12, god-awful, oily gin will do just that.

Why they need to lock up a $12 pint of gin behind four inches of bulletproof glass should be studied by the world's social science community. The secret behind all class conflict and social instability in the Western hemisphere lies within the walls of this American public convenience store.

My mouth begins to salivate, and my head begins to ache at the same time—an immediate conditioned response to the simultaneous reward of getting drunk and the premonition of the morning after.

After completing my purchase, I step outside and see a bum who's bleeding from the mouth and lying on the ground with his hand outstretched towards me. He's pleading for me to "help" him, but I don't know what I can do. His condition seems irreversible. Horrified, I nervously grab a handful of change and a few ones and throw them down onto the ground in front of him before running away like a little bitch. As I power walk my ass back toward the hotel, the gin bottle lightly nudging my leg as I stride, it transforms the usual prospect of drinking into a sense of *urgency*. It is time.

As I come darting through the casino lobby, I quicken my pace in an effort to evade any more horrible images before falling asleep, but it's hard to ignore the post-menopausal woman in a tight pleather miniskirt jacking off an even older man in the corner behind one of the decorative plants. Hand right down his trousers, pumping up and down with great vigor, the man's head tilted back in frugal ecstasy, mouth open, pink and panting for that last bit of inspiration. Where is security for this kind of thing? *Where?*

Rounding the corner toward the elevator, I crack open the gin and take a long, dirty pull. As I enter my room I kick off my shoes and pants, take a seat on the bed, and kill an entire third of the bottle between hard gagging breaths.

I walk over to the bathroom mirror and lift up my shirt. I'm getting fatter. I'm becoming just like everybody else here. Overweight. Unconcerned. Uninterested. *Uninspired*. What a disgusting mess I've become in such a short time—thirty years old and a case of hemorrhoids that would put septuagenarians and power lifters to shame. *How long will it take before the gout kicks in?*

Behind me in the mirror, I see all the tissues and tiny lotion bottles resting next to the remote control on the nightstand by the bed. I walk over, now completely naked somehow, save for a pair of yellowed, week-old socks. I take another long pull of the gin and plop myself down on the edge nearest the TV. I reach for the remote. *HBO.* HBO will make me feel better. It makes everyone feel better. That's why they have it for free in your casino hotel room—so you don't blow your fucking brains out and ruin all the upholstery.

After watching two back-to-back episodes of *Entourage* I feel like snuffing it even worse now, and I have no idea why. Maybe it's the dialogue. Maybe it's because I know I'll never see this kind of life. Maybe it's because I know it's a terrible show, and I'm ashamed that I've somehow been entertained by it for at least two hours.

Fuck. The sun comes peeking through the curtains, and now the Victory Gin is all gone. There's still the mini bar (thank Christ), and I end up finishing six tiny bottles along with several more episodes of *The Wire* and two whole bags of emergency potato chips that I bought at the booze pharmacy, just in case of *right now.*

Suddenly, it's full-blown morning, and I'm so drunk

now that I can't even sleep. I've got the squirms and the spins so bad I feel like I've eaten an entire bottle of baby aspirin—not enough to kill me unfortunately, but enough to feel utterly poisoned. As I lay there drooling on the pillow watching the sun getting higher and higher from the little crack in the curtains, I'm zapped with panic as I realize the housekeeping lady will be knocking on my door in less than four hours, telling me I need to leave. Then I'll have the whole day ahead of me to deal with— trying to play winning poker in a pre-panic, sleep-deprived state; trying to find someone other than Harris to room with tonight; and trying to keep my wits about me and make decisions that won't lose me an unholy amount of money.

This won't work. I cannot deal with these things in such a short time. I desperately need peace. *Convalescence.* In a panic, I find a pen and paper on the nightstand, and thankfully, there's a piece of gum stuck to the underside of it. I use the gum to stick a $50 bill to the back of the Do Not Disturb sign with a little note that reads:

JUST 3 MORE HOURS
THAT'S ALL I NEED
MUCHAS GRACIAS

2

PHILADELPHIA, son.

I decide to stop by the house to check and see if the city's boarded up the windows, or if there's a sheriff's notice pasted to the front door. This is what you expect after the economy shits the bed; you stop paying the mortgage and abandon your home to go dust off what meager savings you had before moving to Atlantic City in an attempt to "play poker for a living." If the property's been officially seized by the bank, I'll be on the next train Westbound for Mom and Dad's—if not, then I'm not sure what I'm going to do. What I left in that place was a fucking disaster almost a year ago.

As I climb the front porch to inspect the façade, I see no immediate evidence that anyone's been here since I left the place. I'm fairly surprised and almost offended that the neighborhood dope fiends or Bank of America haven't seized the property yet.

I cautiously slip the key into the door and open it

wide before stepping in. I yell hello to see if anyone's there. Nothing. No sound or movement at all. *Looks promising.* I stand there in the living room and take a good look around. The place looks exactly the way I left it: a demolition zone. The downstairs is completely gutted to the core. Naked copper plumbing ascends the open walls. Threads of ragged jute are still stapled to rough exposed floorboards. No walls, just the old studs demarking the rooms that used to be here. I feel around for the light switch and then remember that there's no overhead lighting in here anymore either. I tore out all that knob-and-tube shit just weeks before the stock market crashed—never had an *economically viable* reason to replace it after that.

I walk into the kitchen, open the freezer door, and find half a carton of stale smokes I forgot before I left. I step outside to burn one.

No one's in sight, and there are hardly any cars parked along the streets like there used to be. Some city dirt blows by. There's a small pile of chicken bones in the middle of the sidewalk in front of the stoop. No other signs of life. No yelling or screaming like usual. No apeshit pit bulls or ratfink little neighbor kids creeping the corners. I look across the street. The insides of the houses are all dark over there.

I close the door behind me, but this time I stick the key in and lock it before I leave. I'm not really sure why.

Maybe I'll stick around and wait for the bank to come physically remove me from the premises.

I head downtown to get anesthetized.

I really have no business coming back to Philly. I should be heading back home with intentions of finding honest, shit-paying work as soon as I get into town. But tonight is a special occasion; tonight is the three-month anniversary of my first real downswing, which has also just about crippled me. I've been running bad in live poker for almost ninety days.

What does "running bad" mean? It means losing $50,000 in just under three months at middle stakes poker. It means a $2700 chicken sandwich—that's the chicken sandwich you eat right after you've just lost $2700 right before lunchtime.

Running bad means *loss*—of Gatsbian proportions.

But this is what happens when you lose everything in real estate after the global economy crashes, and then try playing poker for a living with what's left of your life savings, even though you don't actually have all that much experience with the game. You *run bad*. It has nothing to do with you or the decisions you make; you're just *unlucky*.

So what now? Get a job at minimum wage? Move back in with the folks and work overtime for five years to save up another minimum bankroll and try it all over again? Or, borrow it from a loan shark at twenty points a week and blow your fucking brains out if you don't win. These are the kinds of thoughts you have when you've lost so much money that you can barely breathe—when you wake up every afternoon choking with panic, the constant din of loss scrabbling under your skin. You get nightmares about losing hands. You get this constant low-fi anxiety humming in the fog of your mind all day and all night while you wonder about all of the things you could've done with all that fucking money you used to have. You start thinking differently, hearing things *differently*. "World News Tonight with Peter D-Jennings"; a Chinese man behind the counter asks you if you want "Donk Sauce"; some weirdo white trash degenerate at the casino bar tells you that when you run really bad for a really long time, you need to do what's called a "luck changer."

"What's a *luck changer*?" you ask him.

"You fuck a black girl in the ass," he tells you. "Then your luck changes."

You used to be the kind of guy who would think, *Jesus man, that's really fucking racist.* Now you're the kind of guy who thinks, *Jesus man, does that shit really work?*

I end up at a bar called McGlinchey's. This is now the only place anywhere near Center City where you can still smoke at the bar. It's the only place where you can get a beer at fair price. It's the only place where there aren't any frat boys and sorority slits barking at the moon. Beers for three dollars, hot dogs for seventy-five cents. No pool tables. No TV. No Megatouch, Quizzo or karaoke. It's just a bar. Just beer and smoke and AC/DC on the jukebox for a few hours on a slow and steady Monday night.

Tonight, everybody normal is asleep because they all have work tomorrow. So everyone here is just like you—unemployed, a little weird, a little broken—which means they're also inclined to leave you the fuck alone. I take a seat at the bar, light up a smoke and order a beer. Beside me is a fairly gross couple necking and petting like children in heat. They look like starved dogs chomping down a bloody breakfast off of each other's faces. You can feel the humidity and almost taste that yeasty beer vapor on their breaths—the dude's rank, shitty cologne wafting into the still, wet air with every groping motion. I want to look away, but I can't.

After about nine or so beers, I see a big-ass white chick with jet-black hair blast through the barroom doors. Black leather, big curls, the kind of woman, I imagine, who likes to be fucked in a German sniper mask. She comes barreling through the room like she owns the place, bellies up to the bar, and takes the stool nearest me.

I have this nasty feeling like something very bad is

going to happen to me tonight. I just know it. I can already see myself groping through the darkness back at the house where there's no electricity—just the blackness and the unknowing and the danger of an abandoned home in a bad neighborhood. But right now, I don't even care. Tonight, I'll be damned drunk enough to deal with it. Tonight, I will cast a deafening white noise over the voice of thought so heavily there will be no room for fear. *Just keep the booze coming, and it'll all be over soon. Just keep drinking, and the dawn and the pain and the sun will all be here before you know it. With the right medicine and the right dosage, anything is tolerable.*

Before I know it, I'm too drunk to understand what's been happening since I got here. I have no recollection of how we started in, or who approached whom, but this woman's been buying me cheap drink after cheap drink, and I'm having mad trouble keeping up with her. Quite frankly, her body mass is considerably more than mine, so she's soaking it all up a lot better than I am. I think she knows this, and she also knows that, as a man, I can't under-consume her for the sake of both our egos—she doesn't want to look like the fat chick, and I don't want to look like a little bitch—so if there's any chance of us fucking each other with any semblance of dignity this evening, I'm just gonna have to *drink up*.

This girl is bigger than I like, and she has this tattoo of a black widow on one of her humungous tits. While she goes to the bathroom to do drugs, I end up ordering six regular hotdogs for myself and one kosher dog for her, just in case. When she finally gets back I've already finished my third, partly because I'm simply a disgusting human being at this point, and partly because I need to metabolize some of this poison she's been feeding me for the last god-knows-how-many hours. But it doesn't seem to help. She keeps ordering drinks, and she ate one of my hotdogs after she finished hers, and now I'm beginning to feel legitimately unwell.

Another hour goes by. Maybe three. Maybe I've been here my whole life. It's hard to tell when you've gotten this drunk this fast for this long. I can't see much past what's directly in front of me, and I can't recall what I've been saying to this person or what's been said to me since we got here. All I seem to remember is some good AC/DC on the juke, some affirmative muttering to whatever we've been on about, and the constant choking down of Wild Turkey, neat, which seems to come with an unspoken sense of urgency every ten minutes. I look at the clock on my phone, which says 9:30 p.m. *How in God's name could it be 9:30 p.m.?* It seems impossible to be this drunk by 9:30 p.m., and now we're LEAVING, but I have no idea why. I've erased all memory for any shortterm plans I might have made to get in bed with this woman.

We've just hit the streets hard and nasty, and I'm

following her around like a lost hungry dog as we walk down some street near Rittenhouse—*Locust* maybe. Then I hear the chirp of a car alarm, and I look behind me to see the parking lights flash on a very well-maintained, clearly garage-kept, 1995 Eagle Talon. *Black*.

She looks at me standing there, wavering back and forth, hot-boxing a cigarette, as I try to jump-start my brain for the deciding moment. I say nothing as I try to think if I even want to do this right now. Then I hear the locks pop. "Get in," she tells me, "let's go for a drive." I get in, and she turns the ignition, puts in a mixed CD labeled with a giant X in black Sharpie. She slips on these shiny black leather driving gloves—the kind with the knuckles cut out. *What the fuck is going on here?* She rolls down all the windows and tells me to "Buckle the fuck up, babe."

The drive to wherever the fuck it is we're going is like that scene in *Charlie and the Chocolate Factory*, where Willy Wonka has everyone trapped on his paddleboat for the electric nightmare chocolate river ride. She's blasting 90's grindcore through a clearly aftermarket stereo system, while wind lashes through the open windows of the Talon. Most of the drive is under the El, and we're surrounded by the dark rusty girders of the subway above. Blowing through streetlights, zipping past glowing neon from the late-night delis and smoke shops, I gather we're headed towards Upper Darby or somewhere inside greater Delco, but I can't find the mental acuity to figure it out or even care enough to confirm it. As time passes, the ride feels more and more like a dream, where the details don't matter much and you never know who or where you are. The only certainty is how powerless you feel against the force of whatever horror is fueling the moment. And then, a quick twinge of panic belts me in the chest as I realize I've almost completely forgotten who I'm with, where I am, or where it is I might be going. For fifteen solid minutes, I've forgotten that another human being, a complete stranger, has been driving me *somewhere*, and now, for the life of me, I can't even remember her name.

Some minutes later, we pull into a driveway and the music stops. I regain some of my consciousness. We step into her house, which is like a real-life *house*, and it's actually pretty nice and normal inside. Not at all like mine, and not at all like the S&M bondage chamber I imagined, judging by the goth freak show I'd just endured inside her car.

I step further inside. She disappears into a dark kitchen, and a bottle of wine materializes. *No. No more. Please!*

She sits us down on the couch and starts saying shit like, "I *seriously* have *never* done this before. This is something I would *never* normally do. I mean, like, pick someone up at a bar and take them into my home like this? Yeesh! This is *so* unlike me."

"Yeah, me too," I say. But I'm actually telling the truth.

And then she says, "I just got, like, so *horny* for no reason today, and I haven't had a good fuck in a while, so I thought *screw it* I'm goin' to the fuckin' bar to find some DICK! Haha! Gawd! Isn't that *awful?*"

YES. Yes, it is.

I put down my glass and move in to eat her face and she follows my lead. After some clumsy necking and grabbing on each other we run up to her bedroom. On my way up the stairs, I trip over a giant plastic child's plaything. I look to my left, the opposite direction she's attempting to lead me, and there's an entire room full of children's toys. *Glorious.* Before I even have a second to register this information and form an opinion about it, she grabs my hands and pulls me toward her bedroom, "It's okay, don't worry," she reassures me. "He's already got a daddy, and you'll never have to meet him."

She makes me help her remove the pink, shiny combat boots she's wearing, and her feet are kind of like right in my face, which I find to be pretty gross. She stands back up, walks over to the light switch and makes it dark before pulling off her dress, but I can still make out her giant baloney tits, the areolas like huge unevenly poured pancakes.

The condom I have turns out to be like three Ziploc

bags thick, so of course I can't feel a fucking thing. Eventually she gets on her knees and bends over for me, which doesn't look good, even in the dark, and she starts screaming all this shit and yelling my name, which, for a moment, panics me because I remember again that I can't remember hers. Then, right in the middle of all of this, she *stops* me by reaching behind her to tenderly grasp my arm, and then she says warmly, "TIM?" So I stop, but I don't respond verbally. I can't really see her face, but I can tell she's looking back at me by the direction of her voice. "Will you fuck me in my ass?"

"Um, no," I tell her plainly, and she casually responds with a perky "okay" and turns back around to face the wall. And there you have it: the three worst things you could say on a casual sexual encounter have now been said: *1) Don't worry he already has a daddy; 2) fuck me in my ass; and 3) NO.*

Thirty minutes later, I still haven't finished. I'm booze-sick and spinning, standing upright as I get my reward for making her come: a shitty condom blowjob while I stare up into the slow ceiling fan for some kind of divine inspiration. *Should I just ignore her and use an older, better memory to help me finish this?* The prospect of ejaculation now feels like a coup de grace. The ceiling fan is hypnotic, and at some point I lose track of time. This might have been going on for an hour ... or maybe just fifteen to twenty minutes? I have no idea. After a while she gives up, doesn't say anything about it, and quietly crawls into bed. Like it's no big deal. Like this kind of shit happens to her all the time. I lay down, sort of beside her, sort of not, resting one foot on the floor in an attempt to make it all stop spinning, as I try to fall asleep and the blue balls quietly creep in.

In the morning, she politely jerks me off, remembering that I never came last night, which is now basically pointless, but it's a nice gesture. After receiving my hand gesture, I go to the bathroom and have the most uncontrollable, insanely explosive bout of diarrhea I've ever had in my life.

Why not?

I know she's still in the bedroom, right outside the door, and it's all one massive symphony of wet trumpets and trombones spraying out of my ass uncontrollably, my head now buried in my hands in humiliation. I can hear her nervously shout from the bedroom, "I … uh … um … I'm gonna go make some breakfast. You take your time in there, and come down when you're ready." *Jesus Christ.*

I eat 2 pieces of bacon next to her in silence, thank her for none of it, and then, for some horrible reason, she decides to get *spontaneous* and pretends to accidentally spill some juice on the floor. *What the fuck is this now?* She grabs a rag and gets down on all fours and sticks her naked ass out at me from under her nightshirt. I can see *everything*: the hair around her asshole, the giant flowering minora, all of it profane and fully exposed in the cold unforgiving morning sunlight. I don't do anything. I just sit there chewing bacon, staring at the wall, pretending like none of this is happening. *It's like she forgot that it was terrible even drunk and with all the lights off, and now she goes and tries this shit? Unreal.* She looks back at me, and I look at her, and I wait for her to realize that I'm not at all going for it, until she runs upstairs to get dressed for work.

She drives me back to Center City in silence and drops me off at the closest Market-Frankford El station, so I can get back to Kensington. She tells me to call her and then speeds off in her shellac Eagle Talon, which I now notice has an aftermarket performance exhaust system and honest-to-God racing rims.

3

Back in this house again.

When you're all alone you don't really see your own drinking problem—not until recycling day—and then it's bottle after bottle after bottle. You peer down into the full blue plastic tub, and it looks like there's been a party over at your place for weeks. But the sad reality is that you're the only one who's been partying in there. All by yourself. Completely alone. No job. No friends. It's just you and an empty dilapidated house and crude, cheap, debilitating liquid entertainment.

I get up at, oh, say, 3 p.m. I put on some black sweatpants—making sure these aren't the ones with the cum all over the front of them—then some black dollar-store flip-flops and a good old-fashioned American wife-beater. I step outside to unload the heavy recycling. I try not to look too closely at it anymore, so I look up and across the street while I unload it onto the curb.

I see the neighbor. I hate the neighbor. The plus-sized

pink wind pants, the urban-themed Looney Tunes t-shirts, her greasy red hair tied back so tight it makes her eyes look Asian. All day she sits out there, slouching into a moldering couch while she smokes Newports, sips cheap homemade cocktails, and slurs obscenities into a cordless landline telephone. *I have no idea who she's talking to.* Never once have we said hello to one another, and I see her almost every day, because she's never *not* out there on that goddamn couch. Every time she sees me from the curb, she rolls her eyes at me like *I'm the asshole* for wanting to fix up a piece of property in her neighborhood. *Maybe I am the asshole.* What else can a man be who signs a sub-prime mortgage for a piece of shit property in one of the worst white neighborhoods in Philadelphia, six months before the real estate market completely shits the bed? I mean, I definitely felt like an asshole after that one.

Goddamn it. This neighborhood's been all but abandoned over the last six months, and of course SHE'S got to be the only holdout. The only neighbor I have left. If I ever need a cup of sugar I'm fucked. Luckily, I don't.

Suddenly, a shirtless eight-year-old child bursts from their front door. He's running around in circles, screaming, high as fuck on energy drinks. He runs over to the edge of the porch with his big green toy laser gun and declares fearlessly to the adult alcoholic stranger emptying heavy glassware onto the curb … "Space *Jam*, NIGGA!"

I walk back into my house, close the door, and lock it.

I step into my demolished kitchen to make my world-famous austerity brunch—*eggs and nothing*. I eat it on top of a piece of plywood resting between two sawhorses, while I drink freeze-dried coffee and watch the ever-disintegrating social conditions of greater America, right outside my front window. I used to look out that window and imagine condos, renovated townhouses, rich hipsters, adjunct professors, personal injury attorneys—all huddled comfortably inside—settling into this Neo-Victorian, city-neighborhood lifestyle. Now I watch an obese degenerate woman slink into the springs of an old sofa, drink ghetto blasters, and eat chips.

I kept telling myself, back before the autumn of '08, that this was what being a pioneer was all about: roughing it, waiting out harsh conditions, and blazing a trail for others to follow. In time, the middle class would be right behind me, ready to help build it up, backing the ramparts, strengthening us in numbers, fueling DEMAND. But someone's gotta go first. Someone's got to step up and dig his heels in. Someone's got to plant himself right in there with the savages and show them that shit's about to change whether they like it or not.

But how's that saying go? *Telling God about your plans is a good way to make him take a shit all over your face?* It's something like that.

Anyways, it's a little after midnight, and I've been drinking slow. I walk out onto the porch for a smoke, and I take a few steps down into the street. At the other end of the block I can see two, almost identical characters—same backwards hats, same baggy-ass pants, long t-shirts down around their asses. They're arguing over *something*. Then, one of them suddenly swings at the other's head and they both take off down the street. The one who's chasing the other runs him down, gets him on the pavement, and plugs him a few times in the face. But it's not clean, methodical punching like you'd expect from someone with a lot of experience; it's more like that up-and-down hammering motion you get from a nervous, bloodthirsty chimp. After a few seconds, he stops pounding on the poor bastard's face, steps off after yelling some shit, and then just walks away. A few seconds later, the one on the ground gets up and walks off in the opposite direction. *Whatever, none of my business.*

I look over at the other side of the block. It's completely pitch black over there. All of the street lights are out on that side and all of the properties are abandoned, so you don't even get a little glow from the living rooms or the upstairs windows like you do on this side. Over there, everything's all burnt down, collapsed, or boarded up—or it's just an empty half-fenced-off lot full of trash, needles, and spent forties. You can't see anything after dark over there, but you know that's where all the real low-bottom shit goes down: ODs; $10, open-air blowjobs; twenty dope fiends all lined up along a condemned, detached brick wall, leaning and staring off into the blackness. You can't see any of it happening this late at night, but you hear things: slow uneven footsteps shuffle against the asphalt; a bottle clumsily rolls down the street; someone angrily mutters nonsense. No police sirens around these parts, *ever*. This is one of those neighborhoods they talk about—so irrelevant in the social hierarchy that even the cops don't come up here for anything short of a baby murdered in a microwave.

I look back across the street at the neighbor's house. Something catches my eye. I can see a bend in the ugly pink blinds, some dark subtle movements happening behind them. *Is this bitch seriously* SPYING ON ME? *What the fuck is* wrong *with her?* I step forward a little and wave at her with my cigarette. *I can seeeeeee you.* The blinds flip closed, and it's dark again. I look back up and down the block. No one's around now. The noises have all stopped. No movements or sounds or proof of life coming from anywhere. I'm all alone out here.

Daylight. This week's been particularly heavy with the glass and aluminum. Today is a good three-and-a-half-minute deposit onto the curbside. There must be fifteen bucks in recycling here.

Jabba the Bitch isn't out there right now, but I can hear her yelling and carrying on inside the house. It's just a little girl out on the porch at the moment, completely unsupervised. She's *shirtless* and sucking on her thumb. She looks down at one of the empty plastic schnapps bottles resting on the porch and then kicks it out into the street. She's got to be at least eight years old.

I can hear Leviathan thrashing inside the house, and all the children are screaming and crying.

"You know we can't afford this kind of peanut butter right now, you fuckin' idiot! What I gave you was enough for everything AND my fuckin' cigarettes! I fuckin' *told* you. What is *this*? WHAT THE FUCK IS THIS? I told you to get the cheap shit!"

I look over at the little girl on the porch and attempt to communicate a deep telepathic message with the eyes: *DO you want me to help you? DO you want me to call Child Services?* She just looks back at me and giggles, pops the thumb out of her mouth, and gives me the finger. *What the fuck?* I give her an incredulous look back, like: *fuck you too … big girls don't suck their thumb … good luck with your first teen pregnancy … little twat.* She keeps giggling, bounces up on her toes, and shouts at me, "Fuck you! *Fuck* you! Hehehehehe!" I pick up my empty blue recycling tub, drag it back inside the house, shut the door, and deadbolt the motherfucker.

It's Saturday afternoon, and today there is going to be a block party. I thought this place was more or less abandoned. Where did these people come from? *Where?* Furthermore, I did not sign off on this shit. You're supposed to get a permit from the city if you want to have a block party, which requires signatures from the majority of homeowners on the street. Technically speaking, the bank now owns this piece of shit I'm currently living in, but still, no "member of the community" ever asked me to sign anything.

I stand there in the upstairs hallway, staring at all of the unopened boxes—all of the nice shit I bought just three weeks before the housing market crashed. It's all been sitting up here collecting dust for almost a year now: the Pegasus 48" x 26" stainless steel medicine cabinet; the Home Decorators Collection REAL MARBLE sink with teak framing; my new fucking THRONE—a brand new, 1.28 gallon-per-flush American Standard Vormax elongated Victorian commode, glazed in fucking PEARL. But the cocksuckers on Wall Street had to ruin it for me. They had to take away every conceivable financial incentive to allow me a fucking Cadillac for a toilet.

You know what? Fuck this! This property doesn't have to remain a ramshackle demolished piece of shit just because there's a "Great Recession" on. Fuck them and fuck the American economy.

I AM GOING TO REBUILD AN ENTIRE ROOM OF THIS HOUSE IN A SINGLE FUCKING DAY. If not for the home equity, then for ME. If the shit's truly going to hit the fan in the next few years, at least I can die with some dignity in my baller-ass bathroom.

I look out the front window again to confirm my reasons for locking down this evening. *Christ Almighty. Just look at her.* She's got on the choice gear for the occasion: the Wal-Mart track pants (the fake Adidas kind with just the two stripes instead of three); some old Jordans with the sides all squeezed out over the soles; and on top, the pride piece—a brand new, triple-XL original Newport polo. The color and design look exactly like a soft pack. She must have smoked a hundred cartons to earn that.

I decide to get a good sustainable buzz going while I rebuild my bathroom—*like a man does.* Within minutes I can hear the Eminem bumping outside my living room window, so I bring up my heavy duty DeWalt worksite radio CD player, turn the station to classic rock, crack open a Lager, and get to work.

Hours fly by as I've got a nice energetic buzz going, sustained by a few smokes here and there. I install the new toilet, and it goes in without a hitch. The classical-modern-fusion sink and medicine cabinet go in next. I'm in there all day, ripping out the old shit, fastening in the new, sweating pipes, and triple checking everything to ensure it's solid to the core. Everything is coming together perfectly.

I'm about to have a practically new bathroom with a state-of-the-art comfort station that can withstand some of the largest, unhealthiest shits in America, and all for less than $1500 in materials and some good old-fashioned American sweat equity. Feels good. Feels *damned good.*

Before I know it, it's just after midnight and my new bathroom is almost completely remodeled. I order some Chinese food and I overeat just a little, so I can really test out my new commode in the morning. I'm just waiting for the enamel to dry in the tub, a coat of paint after the joint compound has been dried and sanded, and she's all done.

I go into the front upstairs bedroom, which I'd originally dubbed the "smoking room," as it was the last room I planned to finish before I sold the place. *I guess now it's going to be a "smoking room" forever.* I close the door and light up another as I watch from my upstairs window the neighbor folk milling around with their open containers and howling at the moon.

Fuckin' Kenzo, man …

Back in the day, Kensington used to be called *the workshop of the world.* Now they call it *the badlands*—a scorched concrete grid of busted out factories, condemned warehouses and boarded up old row homes. Over the past decade these old river wards have been taken over almost entirely by heroin, and most of the buildings around here have been overrun and repurposed as shooting galleries. The kids call them *Abandominiums*. This typically isn't a good reason to buy real estate. But back in 2007, Kensington was rumored as next in line to be absorbed by the recent "Northern Liberties Corridor Expansion"—a new hotspot for gentrification or "urban renewal." I knew the area was rough, but I was anticipating an invisible hand, greater than God's, pushing all those new hipsters and yuppies my way—squeezing out the white trash in its wake, as the upper-middle class emptied from the suburbs and flowed back into the urban mainland. That was of course until Wall Street had its little anal adventure.

Suddenly, I hear a loud rapid chipping sound, like glass cracking, coming from downstairs. I peep my head down from the landing, but I don't see anything out of sorts. And there it is again. And then again, in rapid fire. *Tink tink tink*. It's coming from the living room, which faces the street. I go back into the smoking room and look down onto the street from the upstairs, and I see one of the kids from next door, this one a bit older, with five of his fifteen-year-old *wigger* buddies. They're *shooting* my fucking front windows with a goddamn BB gun. *Little fucking cock goblins!* There's no way in hell I'm going out there, since the natives have all been liquored up for the last twelve hours. Instead, I whip out my phone and within seconds I'm telling the 9-1-1 operator that there's a group of young men on my street, drinking and waving around "some kind of BIG gun."

In less than five minutes, three cop cars pull up—red and blue lights rolling off of the giant two-story contiguous wall of attached homes. Moments later, the cops find the BB gun and all five kids are up against the house, cuffed one by one.

The drunken sow comes barreling out the front door, tits and torso swinging like wrecking balls, and then she hauls off on the kid right in front of the cops. The little fucker's hands are cuffed behind his back, so she really gets in one solid shot right on the kid's temple and he goes down hard, like someone's just hit his "off button." She tries to jump on top of him so she can beat on him some more, but the cops finally move in to break it up and it takes four of them to pull her three-hundred-pound mass off of the poor bastard. "I told you we don't need this shit right now, goddamn you! How you gonna do this shit with your uncle Virgil in jail! How you gonna ruin the goddamn block party! I'm a kill you! I'm a KILLLLL you!" She lunges again, and this time the cops try and hold her back, but she starts fighting them off, and now my eyes are glued to the window.

One of the cops ain't having it anymore, so he plants himself, elbows her square in the forehead, and drops her like the ton of bricks that she is. They've got her now, one cop has his knee pressed right into the center of her back, pinning her fat ass to the concrete as they begin cuffing her while she cries, pleads, and apologizes, but it's too late for any of that now; the paddy wagon's already pulled up to take everyone off to jail. I've since poured myself two new drinks, pulled up a chair to the window, and enjoyed a couple more smokes as I watch them wrap it up. Once the show's over and everyone's been hauled away, I get up and go stand in my new bathroom and admire my craftsmanship. I finish one more drink, punch out my smoke and head off to the most restful sleep I've gotten in ages.

4

Believe me, I held out for as long as I could. Sat tight, drank responsibly every evening in an effort to dissolve the riskier ideas—you know, like going back to AC and dumping what's left of my life onto the felt and into some other asshole's pockets. No, instead I sat back, collected my unemployment, and minded my own goddamn business deep in the white ghettos of West Kensington.

Every day I sat there, at my "desk," in my man robe, sipping mid-shelf cocktails and entertaining myself with AM talk radio and insane conspiracy theory "documentaries" on the internet. I decided I would do this every night until my unemployment ran out, or until the Sheriff finally came to evict me. Then I'd just move on to whatever the hell I could think of next. You know, kind of like a locust.

And, I might have even enjoyed my stay for a good long while too, if it hadn't been for the goddamn flies.

Yes, *flies.*

One rainy evening, a small flood in the neighborhood sent raw sewage gurgling up through the basement's drainage system. The flies showed up a few days later. Billions of the fuckers. Thick black buzzing clouds blocked out the fucking lights. I didn't do much to prevent it from happening. I just kind of left the sewage down there to fester and hoped it would eventually drain back out. Then maybe I could just let it dry and sweep it up later. Basically, I just wanted nothing to do with raw sewage, and I didn't give a shit enough about the property anymore to pay someone to fix something that I was probably going to be abandoning—*yet again*—at some undisclosed juncture.

Apparently, *this* was that juncture.

First, they infested the basement, which I boarded up and sealed off with some plastic sheeting and duct tape, quarantining it from the rest of the house. In some illogical fantasy of irresponsibility, I envisioned that the flies would eat up all the sewage down there, then eventually starve since I'd trapped them. After that, I wouldn't have to deal with any of it.

But then one morning when they made their way up through the heating ducts, I awoke to an awful buzzing sound, and it *wasn't* my alarm clock. I didn't have an alarm clock anymore. I woke up choking for air, and there they were, all crawling and hopping around on my nose and mouth. I ran to the bathroom and dry heaved for a few minutes, drank some water, then threw that up and got dressed.

I took it as a sign. *Pestilence.* It was time to leave this place for good. Flies know. They know when situations have rotted to the core. They're a carrion organism. Having a nose for death has been coded into their DNA for 250 million years. They know the end is coming before it even happens. So, instead of paying someone to vanquish the infestation from my home and restore my basement back to its original state, I packed up an overnight bag with a few black t-shirts—some socks, some underwear—and I walked right out the fucking door. *Same as it ever was.* I didn't even look back to see what I was leaving behind this time: some good-working power tools, a modestly outdated computer, some perfectly working electronics, random personal effects, and documents with my information all over them. It didn't matter anymore. I'd dare anyone to steal my identity now—it was a toxic asset. I didn't even turn off the gas or cancel the electric or the cable this time. I just left it all there, along with most of my valueless belongings. I even left the door wide open, in case any low-bottom dope fiends wanted to repurpose the place as a needle depository—my gift to the neighborhood and the godforsaken American banking system.

I walked to the corner of Kensington and Somerset,

stood under the El and waited for a cab to take me to Center City. Shit. It was already 3 p.m. It was time for a beverage.

Sitting at the bar, I felt an enormous weight of shame and remorse pressing down. I remember thinking about how utterly unsustainable my behavior was. *A person should have to be responsible for what they own and to whom they owe. You can't throw an entire house in the garbage just because it turned out to be more responsibility than you bargained for.* But the truth was, this was America, and you could do exactly that. You could throw your whole home right into the shitter and walk. Literally millions of Americans had already walked away from properties they either could no longer afford, or simply no longer wanted, now that they were worth less than what was borrowed to buy them.

It felt horrible to be part of a broken system, twisting in the wind on the wrong side of history. I felt like I was turning into every douchebag Republican banker who touted deregulation and capitalism with every fiber, and then turned into complete butt-fucking socialists the minute they needed someone to bail them the fuck out. The values of this world of ours were quickly turning into something that was getting harder and harder to take seriously. No one stood for anything anymore, and in some small part, it was because of people like me.

That afternoon the rain subsided, and I left the bar. With nowhere to stay, I decided to take a cab to 30th Street Station. I stood in the middle of the station, watching the cities and departure times appear and reappear on the split-flap board. Nineteenth-century technology ticking and flapping away in a train station seemingly as old as America herself. DC. Baltimore. Schenectady. New York. I knew not a soul in any of these places. What was the point of going anywhere? How different could my situation be in any of these places compared with right here and now?

And then I saw it.

ATLANTIC CITY. 6:30 p.m.

Goddammit.

So that was it. That's all it took. I was going back. But this time I decided, right off, that there would be *no poker*. I'd get a free room for a couple nights, sure, but just to relax. No business. *Just grind some penny slots in exchange for some watered-down drinks, mill around the casino, watch a little TV in the hotel room, enjoy a little room service, and take it easy for a couple days while I plan out what to do next.*

At that point I could have really used some amenities anyhow. I'd been squatting in my own home for the past six months.

Yeah, AC would be good this time around. A nice semi-clean room for a couple nights, and a good steak dinner (courtesy of the Commonwealth of Pennsylvania). Shit, maybe I'd get lucky and win the fucking jackpot. This was a great idea. What could be better at this moment in time, under these specific circumstances? Just a couple relaxing days in Atlantic City, get my shit situated and then get the fuck out of New Jersey. Maybe forever this time.

5

When I arrive at the Borgata, I'm immediately seated in the five-ten no-limit game, the biggest they have going right now. I look around the room for Harris. No sign of him anywhere—probably off stuffing this afternoon's winnings into some hooker's ass. Maybe I'll catch up with him later.

As soon as I sit down, I notice the game is packed with obscene action. There's so much money on the table that it almost offends me. Half of the players are drug dealers, a couple of nit-bastard grinders I recognize from a while back, *and fucking Brian.* Brian: the world's most inconspicuous loan shark. This guy's a fucking trip—a real New-York-literary-Jewy-looking dude. Not tall. Cardigan. Horn rims. *Very* tall hair. For some reason the movie *Weird Science* always comes to mind when I see him. The man actually carries an artisanal leather-bound *ledger*—like the kind an accountant would carry before the internet.

"So good to see you again," says Brian, giving me a warm inviting smile. "Glad to see you're back on your feet."

If by "back on your feet" you mean buying in to the biggest game of your life with the last two thousand dollars to your name, well, then, THANKS!

"Thanks," I tell him, "it's good to see you too." I order a Black Label and causally fold jacks to a 4-bet, as I watch my set hit the flop and three players frantically jam all of their chips into the center of table. Off to a great start.

Long story short, in less than two hours I'm drunk and heads up with this white-trash drug dealer from Northeast Philly. I think I've seen this asshole on my block before. When he sat down, I noticed he was wearing a diamond-studded belt buckle in the shape of a human skull. *What the fuck is wrong with people today?* He's got a black Phillies cap on, and he's got one of those thin chinstrap beards. I fucking hate those.

Anyways, I just flopped top two on a dry board. He leads into me with a massive over bet, so I ship it in his face. He snap-calls and the dumb bastard turns over a bottom pair. He shows it to me like, "Yeah bitch, I don't even give a fuck." A wave of relief washes over me. My hand is a fucking monster against this ass clown.

The turn is a blank, and I exhale another small sigh of relief. *Just one more pull, two outs to fade, and I'm home free. I'll* *have over four grand. That's enough for a down payment on a new, used car. Or maybe I'll just snap-rack after this and drop down to $1/2 No Limit and start grinding again. Maybe this is where shit finally starts to turn around.*

The dealer casually pulls the river, and suddenly there's this queer, sharp sting that resonates through my face, neck, and fingers. There are no words or thoughts, just that shock and buzz that comes with real trauma. I see his third six wobbling there at the far-right end of the board from where the dealer just fucked me in my fucking asshole. It's hanging there like twelve inches of black cock in an eighth grade boys' locker room. Devastating.

I tell him "nice hand," and quietly get up to leave the table. He doesn't say anything or even look up at me—just drags it all in like he doesn't give a shit about winning a $4000 pot—like he somehow deserves it. I can see Brian out of the corner of my eye, offering a twisted facial expression like he's just witnessed an industrial degloving injury, but I can't even meet his eyes. I just turn around and walk away.

I head back to my room to go lie down.

As soon as I get back to my suite, I order every bottle my credit will allow from the room service menu. *Tonight, I'm going to drink until my heart stops.*

Within minutes they send me up some skinny punk with an eyebrow ring, who wheels in all my mid-shelf liquor on a black felted table. I inspect it silently, as I run through a tab I have no intention of paying. Then the kid says to me, "Did ya hear Green Day's coming this weekend? I'm going," he tells me proudly. "I got great seats too. Do you like Green Day, sir?"

I smile psychotically at him and reply, "Oh, yes. They're *quite* the artists." Then I crack open one of the Bacardis and slam it straight from the bottle, right in front of him. He leaves immediately without another word.

Yeah, I drink it all. I mix the clear with the brown and everything in between. Fast and dirty, I drink it down.

But the reality of it is, it's actually pretty hard to drink yourself to death in a single evening. Your body kicks it back up pretty good, and with this I end up puking twice before I no longer have the gumption to keep going. No, I won't be dead tomorrow, which means I'll be stuck with the room service bill and no more money and nowhere to go.

After about six more hours of trying to blind myself, I plod my way to the bathroom, as it seems the safest, most logical place to have a seriously dark moment. I end up sipping lightly now, on the toilet, alone in the dark, with only a little sliver of moonlight coming in from the suite's panoramic gold-tint windows. I sit there, and I drink. I try to forget about the house; about the dying job market awaiting me after all of this; about Atlantic City and what a stupid fucking idea it was to try and play poker for a living, after already having lost nearly everything else. It's all enough to drive a man to murder. And now, there are no distractions available to me anymore, because I can no longer afford them.

As the sun eventually begins to peek through the vertical fold in the blinds, I try to remember what the fuck went wrong: how I managed to flush over $50,000, how I managed to gain thirty pounds in a single year, how I've somehow changed my body's chemistry to become so dependent on caffeine and alcohol that water now tastes like poison.

I take another swig from the bottle.

Goddamn it. I should've stopped in the middle when things started to get bad. I'd still have about twenty-five grand. I could've done something with that.

And now, I'm approaching that point where that last drink puts me right over the edge. *Dipsomania. Insane drunk.* I slam the last four or five ounces of swill and stare at the bathroom sink cabinet. A completely functional bathroom cabinet and an honest-to-god marble sink, not unlike the one I put into my own bathroom just a few months back.

I haul off and kick a hole right into the center of the cabinet, smashing it into toothpicks. I stand up and throw the empty bottle at the mirror and it all comes cascading down like a blanket of shimmering sand. I punch a hole in the wall beside me. And another, and another.

Those last few ounces creep up on me hard. I start to feel those dark heavy curtains of a deep blackout drunk coming down. I've got those fuzzy doubles in my vision. Everything starts spinning. I fall back down onto the toilet seat. And just as clear and as certain as I was once here, I'm gone.

That morning I dreamt of bedlam. Global collapse. I dreamt of urban structure fires so vast they bent out into the horizon. I saw mobs looting super markets and home improvement centers for batteries, canned goods, and bottled water. I saw Eastern European cities alight with chaos. I saw bridges aglow with flames so tall they licked the sky. There were young people masked in rags, jumping up and down like rabid apes on burning automobiles. I saw dumpster fires, border blockades, riot police in city centers; I saw gases and smoke of all colors; snipers on rooftops and secret police murdering civilians in the shadows and alleyways behind half-demolished tenement buildings. I saw entire nations on the brink of starvation; masses of naked savage people running mad onto the frontiers of neighboring countries like herds of thirsty insane elephants. I saw the end mounting. Alarm bells were ringing ... ringing and ringing.

The next thing I know, I'm awakened by my phone. Blunt pain comes bludgeoning down over my eyes. My back is so stiff from passing out upright on the toilet that my vertebrae feel fused together. There's that horrifying awareness you encounter when you wake up and you're still drunk: the aesthetics of a perverse and magical evening, all gone, now only the negatives of impairment, the skull filled with molten lead and that scorched hollowed-out burn of oncoming panic buried somewhere in the low center of the ribs. I can hear the blood, thin as water, swirling around in my ears. I look down at the caller ID. It says the words:

SHYLOCK BRIAN

What the fuck?

I instantly throw up into the marble sink that I just destroyed a few hours ago, and it comes out splashing all over the shards of broken mirror. After I finish, I wonder for a second, *am I going to get arrested for this, or just billed?* I answer my phone before the last ring.

"Hey bro," a voice calmly says to me.

I look at the digital clock over there on the nightstand. It says 9:03 AM. *Jesus Christ, what kind of criminal gets up before noon? A Jewish one, I guess.*

I attempt to say "Hello" back in an undamaged manner, but it comes out all ragged and phlegmy.

"Are you ok? You sound like you just threw up or something?"

"I'm *fine*. What is it, Brian?"

"Well, I guess I'll get right to it then. Uh, how do I put this? I noticed you haven't been *running too good* these days."

"YES! AND?"

"Well, I think I might be able to help you."

"Look man, I already told you, I'm not interested in a *street* loan."

"Oh, oh, no. Oh, no, no." Brian laughs nervously, "It's nothing like that. And can we just *take it easy* with that kind of language while we're on the phone, please?"

"Right ... Sorry," I tell him

"Anyways, I might have a gig coming up, that's all. Something nice and soft that'll *definitely* help you get back on your feet."

"Who says I need to get back on my feet?"

"Come on, *bro*. I saw what happened last night. Nobody takes *one* shot and then leaves a game like *that* unless they're flat fucking busted."

I pause for a second to consider this observation. He's right, though I admit nothing.

"Listen, man. Just meet me at the buffet in twenty minutes," and then he hangs up the phone.

I love the Borgata breakfast buffet. Total comfort. But I can't imagine eating or drinking anything right now. All I want to do is crawl into a hole with no light or sound, where it's cool and quiet and earthy inside, and just fade away. But I have to leave this place soon for fear of prosecution, and now I have nowhere to turn back to. I can't even afford a train ticket back home—not until next Wednesday, when my unemployment clears. *Thank God for direct deposit; I don't even have a physical mailing address anymore.*

I hop into the shower. I sit down in the tub and let the hot hard rain pour down on my aching, disgusting, naked body. I look down at myself, my fat little man tits spilling out over my round belly—not unlike a Buddha statue, but with plenty of hair and no jewelry. *What the fuck have I been doing to myself?*

At this point, I have a pretty good idea why Brian has contacted me, and it isn't good. He knows I'm tapped. He personally witnessed me take the ball-beating of a lifetime six months ago when I was still living here. So now he's come up with some kind of dangerous, illegal odd job for me to perform, and he knows I'll probably do it because I have no other options. This is generally how the real world works; people with money never get fucked because there are so many shit heels and mopes with no options to pile high and deep onto the front lines. This is where I fit in now.

I meet Brian at the buffet line just before 10 a.m. We're both late, and neither of us says a word to one another. We're both clearly hung over. He's wearing sunglasses, and I'm closing my eyes and rubbing the pain from my temples as we stand and wait behind 50 senior citizens under the cold, brutal cafeteria lighting. Finally, we're seated, and Brian goes and gets fruit and an English muffin. I come back with double-battered French toast stuffed with scrapple and a side of bacon. We sit in silence nursing our beverages. After a few bites, he finally says something.

"So, I've got this thing for you ... *maybe*."

"Oh yeah?" I say, feigning disinterest, as I salt and sugar my meal.

"I want you to run a two-five game for me in New York."

I pause to consider this rather abrupt, though not at all surprising proposal. What he's talking about is running an underground card game. This is of course, *illegal*, and I assume dangerous. I say nothing in response as I stab at my meal and let him finish his little pitch.

"I know it's within sort of a legal *gray* area," Brian says, making these high obnoxious air quotes with his hands, "but it's good money and the penalty is a chicken-shit misdemeanor, so if don't have any priors, well, let's be honest, you're *white*, so don't even worry about it."

I pause from sipping my coffee and raise an eyebrow at him.

"*Anyways*, it'll help you rebuild your roll and get back on your feet."

"Where in New York?" I ask this as if knowing would actually mean something to me.

"*Manhattan.* Hell's Kitchen, actually. I got a whole new Midtown operation running as we speak."

"So what do you need me for?"

"Well …" He pauses and sighs as he rubs obvious irritation from his temples. "I got a couple of guys there now that *need to go.* And, quite frankly, you refused me for a loan a while back, which to me means you're smarter than most of the people who have enough experience with this game to actually run one. Basically, I need someone who's intimately familiar with poker and who isn't a complete piece of shit, or just an out-of-control degenerate fucking gambler." He looks me deep in the eye. "Men of this ilk aren't that easy to come by."

"Well, thanks for the vote of confidence, but I don't know. I mean, no offense, but it sounds a little shady."

"Listen, why don't you just try it out for a few weeks, and if you decide you don't like it, I'll just find somebody else. No strings. Trust me." He leans in and whispers, "We're talking low risk with *a lot* of upside here."

I say nothing in response and nervously move my food around on my plate.

"So how much do you chop in a game like this?" We're talking about the rake now—how Brian makes money off of the game—the illegal part.

"Ten points up to twenty-five bucks, and fifty at a thousand or more."

"Wow! What a fucking rip-off."

"Yeah, but that's standard for city games. *New York* is a fucking rip off, bro," again with the fucking air quotes. "But if that's what the market bears, then so be it." Brian leans in deeper and starts whispering heavily now for some reason. "Listen! It isn't our responsibility to run games that people can *beat*, Tim. It is our responsibility, *to ourselves*, to make money in exchange for providing *illicit* entertainment to the public."

I stop eating and look at him for a few seconds. This guy is something else.

"I dunno, man. Isn't this whole underground gambling scene kind of like *mobbed up*? Isn't some goon going to come and like *shake you down* if they get wind that you're doing this shit in their *territory*, or whatever?"

"Come on, *bro*," Brian leans back in his seat and shoots me a condescending look. "What decade do you live in? This isn't the nineteen *seventies*, man. Giuliani cleaned up the city like ten years ago. It's like fucking Disneyland now. Any *mafia* is deep in the outer boroughs. Manhattan is an *open city*, my friend. And with all these Wall Street jackoffs out of work now, a lot of them are trying to play poker for a living with their severance packages. I'm *telling* you, the market is *ripe* for action. Anybody can do this shit. There are games all over the city."

"So what exactly is your edge if there are games all over the city?"

"Well," Brian leans back and spreads both arms across the seatbacks beside him, smirking at me like he's got some kind of inside tip. "It just so happens that New York has an underserved market for *non*-ghetto-ass card games. You should see the average one-two scene over there; it is—how do I say this—*parsimonious* as fuck. And with my schedule in Jersey these days, I can't be there to babysit motherfuckers all the fucking live long day while I got shit going on all over the place. So, what I need is a *guy*—like a *solid* GUY—who can help us run a nice clean operation, and who can keep the whole thing nice and *tight*. Ya feel me?"

I look back at him, but choose not to respond.

"Listen." He leans in and starts whispering again. "Even a one-table two-five game in the city grosses over five hundred an hour."

Five hundred an hour. Damn. If I could even get ten percent of that it'd be more than I was ever making on my own. Which was nothing. But still.

I look up at Brian and take in a long deep breath.

"Fuck it. When?"

"Great!" he says, as he smacks the table with conviction. "*Listen*, do you know how to deal?"

"Sure," I tell him. The truth of course is that I've never dealt a single hand of poker in my life.

"Great! I'll inform our *friends in Wilmington* that we've got some fresh blood on this thing. They'll be pleased.

Some of these clowns I've got working up there now have been making me *uncomfortable* for quite some time."

"You have partners in Wilmington?" I ask, a little confused, as I don't really know who or what he's talking about.

Brian shoots me a cold, dead-serious look, like I should definitely be understanding his weird nebulous code-talk. "Uh, *yeah*," he sneers. "And so do you now."

"All right," I tell him.

"Okay, listen," he says. "I'm going to need you there, like, *today*." He tells me this rather causally as he looks down and starts texting some shit into his phone. "I'll meet you in the West Village later this afternoon. I want you to come on some errands with me, then we'll head uptown to where the game's at. Right now, I've got to take care of a couple things before I go. Meet me *here* at 3:30 p.m." Brian texts me a time and address.

"Today?" I ask him, absolutely horrified by the prospect of doing anything today.

"*Yes*, today! Do you have something *else* going on that I'm unaware of?" This is obviously rhetorical. "Take a couple of hours to get your *shit* in gear and meet me in fucking New York. The job starts *to-day*!"

He stands up, leaving an untouched breakfast on the table. He straightens himself and buttons the gay little wooden toggles on his tastefully green, light-weather jacket and then slips back on his Tom Ford wayfarers. He then bends down to *whisper* in my ear: "Crime *pays*, bro," he says darkly, as he lightly squeezes my shoulder. "Don't let them bullshit you."

6

It's 3:00 p.m., and here I am aboard one of the slowest moving passenger trains in the free world. I had to come all the way back to Philly just to take the godforsaken Amtrak because Greyhound from AC to New York was delayed indefinitely after one of their inbound rigs capsized and slid into a stanchion at sixty miles per hour. The crash peeled back the entire roof like a fucking sardine can. Apparently, half of the passengers were decapitated. Hence the delay.

My eyes and head burn, my mind is a piece of shit, and my resolve is fragile and arguably dangerous. I've been dealing with one of the worst hangovers of my life for the past six hours, and now there's no time left to sleep off any of it, as our antiquated locomotive begins its slow fibrous grind through the bowels of Penn Station.

As I deboard, some demented old bat has the *balls* to offer me her copy of the *New York Times*.

"Oh, did you want today's paper? I'm all finished with

it."

I see what she's doing; trying to pawn off the responsibility of recycling her reusable paper waste on some poor unassuming sap like myself.

I look her deep in the eye. "I don't *read*," I snarl in the most condescending tone I can muster.

"Oh," she replies, looking down sheepishly at her newspaper, like it's suddenly been made valueless right before her eyes.

As I step off the train and onto the platform, the first written message I see is:

WELCOME TO NEW YORK CITY
THANK YOU FOR NOT SMOKING

As I take in my surroundings I realize immediately that I look like a homeless person by comparison—a moderately unkempt beard, unseasonable coat, black t-shirt, $30 pants, and extremely practical-looking shoes. I can see already that practical-looking shoes are frowned upon here. On my shoulder is a giant duffle with everything I own stuffed inside. I look like a white refugee. When I step out of the station I get into a cab and the driver takes one look at me and says, "You're not going to Queens are you? I don't go to Queens." I explain to the man that I have no idea where or what the fuck *Queens* is, and I give him an address for somewhere in the West Village. He looks back at me and shrugs. "All right," he says. But he says it with this caveat in his tone, like

Okay, but you're probably not gonna like it.

$23 later I step out onto the streets and begin waiting for Brian. He's late, so to kill time I sit on a park bench and gawk at young NYU girls as they pass. I can't help but *stare*. I'm not at all used to this sort of thing. So many perfect looking girls. In Philly, I used to constantly find myself at the bar playing "Mrs. Potato Head"—putting this girl's face with that one's ass and this one's tits. Here there isn't a single unfuckable girl in sight. *What is this place?*

Suddenly my phone chimes with a text from Brian ordering me to meet him on the south side of Washington Square Park in five minutes. He tells me it's "collection day."

When I show up he's already there, sitting on a park bench and sipping a cortado. "Collection day," which I immediately associate with some kind of criminal violence, apparently instead calls for the gayest cream-colored cardigan I have ever seen in my life and suspiciously tight, raw Japanese denim. Beside him rests an artisanal, handmade Gfeller document case.

He looks up from his phone and smiles. "Wassup, *bro*?" He pops up from his bench and begins walking in the opposite direction looking back at me, and then to his left and right: "Let's go get that money, my *nigga*!"

Jesus Christ.

The first place we go is somewhere nearby. We sneak in to a five-story brownstone apartment building behind some busy ponytailed chick in her gym Spandex. We catch the door behind her and slip into the lobby undetected. Not that it would matter—Brian just looks like another one of her harmless gay neighbors.

We climb a few flights of stairs and stop at number 17. Brian says, "Let me do all the talking. Just hang back. *Take notes.*" Brian knocks on the door, lightly but persistently, for several seconds. Then some Korean kid answers the door in his sweatpants.

"I don't have it," he tells Brian, immediately. "I'm so, *so* sorry, Brian. But I don't have it."

"Listen to me, man. You *gotta* fucking *get it.* Do you understand how serious this is?"

The kid lowers his head and looks submissively at the floor.

"I need to you understand something, Jiwoo; at this point, it's got to be by *any means necessary.* This is the last time I will be paying you a *friendly* visit."

The kid looks up and just stares back, weary-eyed and defeated. He offers a painful exhaustive sigh.

"I'm not saying this to scare you, Jiwoo. But the money you owe isn't to me, do you understand?"

The kid nods, but I can tell he has no idea what Brian's talking about. *I* have no idea what Brian's talking about.

"That money you owe," and now Brian's doing his creepy lean-in-and-whisper thing, "that money you owe is to people you NEVER want to meet, bro. And if they have to come here to get it, believe me, they're going to take a *hell of a lot more* than just their money from you." Brian gently grabs the kid by both shoulders. "Jiwoo, do you understand what I'm saying?"

The poor bastard nods his head frantically up and down, shaking his little brains inside.

"I'm trying to help you, Jiwoo. You gotta get that money. Call your parents. Call a rich uncle. Whatever you gotta do. Believe me, any consequence that you have to endure by telling your family you've been gambling again, it's *nothing* compared to what happens to you if you don't pay these people."

Brian places his hand gently on the kid's back and pulls him in close. "These men are *evil*, bro. They don't care if you're a nice young guy who goes to NYU. They don't care who your family is. These people are *everywhere*. They know *everything*. You can't hide from them. You *gotta get that money*, man. This is your last chance. I'm seriously *afraid* for you at this point."

"Okay, Brian. I'll call my parents. Just a couple more days, PLEASE! PLEASE, just a couple of more days. I will get you the money."

"Okay." Brian fakes a huge sigh of relief. "I believe

you, Jiwoo. I believe that you understand how serious this is. I'll give you another week. But if I come back here next Friday and you don't have it, I won't be able to help you anymore."

"I understand now, Brian. I'll get you the money. I promise."

"I hope so, man," Brian says with a grave and concerned look as he lowers his head. "Good luck to you."

We step outside, and Brian lights up an American Spirit.

"Was any of that true?" I ask him.

Brian laughs at me, "Nah, bro. Are you kidding me? But kids like that'll believe anything. NYU Koreans are a big part of our business. It's illegal for them to gamble back home, so when their parents let them off their leash here in New York, they go straight for the underground card rooms. Most of them are rich as fuck, so it's very good business for us. I don't know what is with those people over there. It's like, to be considered a *real man* in Korea you have to get into some kind of gambling-related trouble. It's like a right of passage or something. Weird culture. But hey, never fuck a gift-horse in the mouth, am I right? Come on. Let's go eat something. I'm fucking *starving*."

We hop into a cab, sit and enjoy the gridlock in silence for about ten minutes while Brian's busy texting on his phone. Then, out of nowhere, he starts yelling at our cab driver. Something about, "I fucking *told you* to avoid Meat Packing."

I look to my right and there's a department store, full of last season's perfumes, sunglasses, handbags, and other bullshit splayed all over the shelves. We sit in traffic as I watch forty or so well-dressed professional adults rifle through last season's discounted merchandise like it's canned goods and bottled water the night before a hurricane.

Brian looks over to see what I'm looking at. "Yeah, they're fucking animals here. You should see how these people play cards. It's like they're *allergic* to money. You're gonna love it here, bro."

Then Brian starts screaming at this poor Indian bastard cab driver again. "PULL THE FUCK OVER! You fucking *incomp*. We're getting out! No tip for you!" he says in a mock Indian accent.

"Jesus Christ, man. Just take it easy."

"Don't take this asshole's side!" Brian hisses, then peels off a few bills from his enormous roll, crumples them up in his fists, and throws them down onto the backseat of the cab.

"You *cannot* let these fuckers hustle you. They will fuck you over every chance they get. Come on, follow me."

We go eat ramen at a place that's packed to the gills with what seems to me like intensely irritated people. We're crammed in there with them, and all the seats are taken, so we're forced to sit at this window bar where everyone's slouched over stools, shoulder-to-shoulder, slurping it up like the unwashed masses. Then, the worst song in American history comes on the radio, which no one seems to notice, and it suddenly occurs to me that maybe New York really isn't for everyone—me included.

After sucking down our soup in less than ten minutes, we begin making our way farther uptown.

After a twenty-minute powerwalk through a gauntlet of tourists along Eighth Avenue, we stand outside yet another five-story walk-up. It's my first night in town, and I haven't slept since passing out on a casino hotel room toilet earlier this morning. Now Brian tells me that there's work available here, *tonight*.

Brian rings a buzzer mounted on the building's wall. After a few seconds, a Russian voice through the intercom answers, "Who is it?"

"It's me, Brian." There's no response, but the door makes a soft humming sound, and Brian pushes it open.

As we walk up to one of the units on the ground floor, there's a subtle click at the door, and Brian opens it without using a key. Once we're inside, there's a little foyer ending at another door—this one nondecorative, metal, and with a heavy-duty electromagnetic lock mounted at the jamb. Brian looks up into a camera above us, and a little light goes from red to green. Brian pushes open the door, and suddenly that nauseating all too familiar sound of clacking casino chips cuts through the air. A dealer calls out the action. SportsCenter whispers highlights on a sixty-inch flat screen. Otherwise, the room is almost silent.

I look over to examine the table. Jesus Christ. It's *Harris*. He's in the dealer box pushing a pot to some Asian kid wearing a $2000 suit. I catch his eye and nod to him casually, and he does the same—like this is a totally normal spot for us to be seeing each other again. I never thought I'd see Harris on the other side of the felt— dealing the cards instead of peeling them. I guess this is what happens to all of us when we go broke gambling; we move to the city to work illegally for people like Brian.

Harris looks different now that he's here in the big city. No more Phillies cap. No more Rocca Wear jeans. He's all dolled up with some good pomade, and he's got on a much nicer shirt than what I'm used to seeing. Apparently, we have some catching up to do.

I look around. This place is actually pretty impressive.

Brian's transformed this little ground-floor residential studio into what seems like a well-organized, single-table Hold 'Em operation. Two dealers, one floor man, ten moneyed, white-collar degenerates with their fucking ties still on. Two more identical corporate shills are rail-birding it in the corner of the room, biting their nails in anticipation as they wait impatiently for a seat to open. All of this is crammed into a 400-square-foot studio apartment.

Brian's floor man is standing at the cage and hasn't said a word since we've walked in. His name is Matt and he's Russian, but he's one of those Kazak-types who looks almost Asian until he says something, and then you hear it: that cold, gloomy Siberian accent. Boredom and disinterest sweat from the man's eyes—like he's been standing at that cage for a decade. Shit, for all I know, maybe he has.

Suddenly, a short, fat, brown guy emerges from the bathroom, followed by an impressive stink. "Fuckin' IBS," he says to no one, to everyone. From the look of him, I think he's some kind of ethnic Gypsy—he appears Indian or Bangladeshi, but he's got that Gypsy swag, even the single gold loop earing. Matt starts staring him down as he approaches us. I'm not at all sure what's going on here, but I feel like something fucked up is about to happen.

Once the Gypsy nears, he reaches in to grab a deck of

cards from the cage, but Brian stops him and asks to have a word in the smoking room. After about a minute, there's suddenly a lot of muffled yelling back and forth from behind the door. None of the players react at all, and Matt just sighs exhaustively. The Gypsy suddenly barges out of the room in a huff, looks me in the face, and shakes his head in disgust, before grabbing his coat and storming out of the place.

Brian comes out after finishing his cigarette, gives me a little half-assed introduction to everyone in the room and grabs a fat little envelope from Matt. "All right everyone, good luck with Tim. *Tim*, good luck with them," and then he leaves me in the room with these people.

And so, I stuff my one big bag containing everything I own into the room's only closet and get ready to jump into the box to deal my first hand of Hold 'Em.

This is my new job, and this place is my new home. Brian's letting me bivouac here until I get my shit together. I will work here every day, and I won't be able to shower or go to bed until the game breaks, every night. The couch where everyone rests their moist, tight asses while they impatiently wait for an open seat will be where I rest my head at night, and I'll be sharing what's essentially a piss-soaked public bathroom with some thirty strangers on a daily basis. This is where I will shower, shit, and brush my teeth every day. This is my new home and my new life. And although conditions such as these might seem aversive or unimaginably uncomfortable to someone of American middle-class upbringing, I feel like this is actually pretty standard for most young people who first move to New York City. But then again, I'm really not all that young anymore.

7

I wake up at 3 p.m. on a fake leather couch. I put my pillow and sheet back in the closet and head outside for breakfast at the gourmet Super Deli on 42nd Street. I come back in, roll out a few napkins on the rail, and turn on the Bloomberg. I listen to plans for the city over the next ten years. More big business is on its way, more tax benefits for startups, more condos, more police, more security surveillance. They're building it bigger, building it higher, building a *safer* more *upscale* city in which to work and live. No one seems to notice or care that the rest of the nation is flat fucking busted. New York City marches on.

Once the coffee loosens everything up, I take anywhere between two, to two-point-five liquid, burning, alcoholic shits. A little sweat. A little more coffee. A little more misinformative television. Then it's time to get to work.

Since I live here now, Brian pays me to clean the

place before every game. It's not a bad arrangement: free NYC rent, plus a little extra cash to do some bitch work on the side. Brian used to hire an honest-to-god, non-English-speaking maid for this shit. But I stole her fucking job at forty bucks a pop because I exercise white privilege whenever humanly possible these days. Can't afford not to.

First I start with the table. I stack the chairs in the corner to give myself plenty of room, so I can get in there and give it a good hard scrub. Everyone's semen, shit, and pissed-soaked hands nervously stroking the felt all night long—shuffling their chips, fondling their money, coughing, eating, sneezing, picking their noses in front of nine other men—all of it gets rubbed down deep into the felt every night. So, I get in there with a nice hot rag, and I scrub that shit down.

Then the chairs are next. Lord knows some of these people have open hemorrhoidal lesions, or perhaps don't wipe their asses all that well (we *do* live in the cultural epicenter of the world, after all), so I use Clorox wipes on the chairs. Then, it's on to the cup holders. The cup holders are situated inside of the padded arm rail for the purpose of placing beverages. Or to throw your garbage. Or spit into if you didn't like that kind of candy. Or to deposit a dirty tissue. *Or,* if your complementary bag of nuts also contains raisins, and *you don't want any of those fucking raisins,* you put those in the cup holder too. By morning they've turned back into grapes. Anyways, all this shit needs to be cleaned up, and I'm the one who gets it done.

Then, I vacuum the 13' x 18' generic Persian rug situated beneath the table. You'd be amazed at what you find under a card table after a hard, thirteen-hour, soul-crushing game. Chips. Change. Wallets. Work IDs. Bundles of keys. Candy. Headphones. Business cards that were distributed at the game. (Some guy hands another guy his business card; the guy accepts it, smiles, and throws it right onto the fucking floor). *One Hundred Dollar Bills*. One time, I found a single men's dress shoe. That one had me thinking for a while.

For the bathroom I use Lysol. I use only hospital grade disinfectant, because it's the only thing that gets the job done right in a place like this. The toilet needs an industrial grade scrub *every day* and for reasons that should be obvious at this point. After cleaning the bowl and the seat, I take old Clorox wipes I previously used on the chairs, and I use them to wipe up all the pubes and piss off of the bathroom floor. Once every square inch undergoes a hospital-grade disinfection, I go out into the main gaming area and I douche it all down with about thirty seconds of air freshener, because in less than two hours this place will be full of complete strangers who have come to this midtown residential studio apartment with the intentions of gambling their fucking faces off, and they sure as shit will be paying out the ass for it, so they only deserve the very best.

8

THE VIGORISH, bro.

It's like this. The chips move back and forth all night long, and all night long we rake the money off of the table, little by little. In this context, the word "rake" is not a term used to describe a horticultural implement—i.e. a long-handled tool used for gardening or the gathering of leaves. Rather, it can be imagined—as Brian has described to me on many occasions—as a "Jew Claw" used for gathering up money off of a table that is felted.

The Rake is a process, it is a strategy, it is a course of action for conducting business. It is in fact a bold-faced term listed in the glossary of the *American Gaming Association's Best Practices* handbook. The Rake is how we, and many other enterprises, both legitimate and illicit, make money from running a poker game. Every time players put money into the pot, the dealer takes a percentage of that pot and drops it into a till. Much like the way your broker or your E-trade account takes a commission on the exchange of securities, the rake is a commission on the action in a poker game. But operations like ours aren't exactly regulated, so we can basically take whatever the fuck we want, which happens to be ten percent of every pot up to twenty-five dollars, and fifty bucks on any pot over a grand. This is of course a fucking rip off. And it happens *every hand*; hundreds of times per night, thousands of times per month. If the action is deep and the game pace is moving along at a decent clip, we're pulling almost one player's average buy-in off the table every hour.

And *this* is how you can make real money in poker. Playing the game in an effort to make a substantial living is an absolute pipe dream. Less than ten percent of all players win long-term, and the overwhelming majority of those who do win aren't capable of winning enough to earn even a teacher's salary on a full-time basis.

In our little rip-off-theater down here in Hell's Kitchen, your chances are even worse. Because even if you are talented enough to beat your opponents, you still have to beat the rake. This will likely amount to about ten percent of approximately half of all the pots you'll ever win. In other words, it doesn't matter how good you are. Eventually, you will lose just like everybody else—only slower.

Then, after having lost nearly everything else, will come the day you lose your fucking mind, and you find yourself borrowing money from someone like Brian, at twenty points a week. *Just a temporary loan—just enough to float you until you get over that little hump.* And then, before you know it, months have passed and you're so buried in *vig* that you're jammed up beyond salvation. The bank accounts, empty. The cash advances, maxed. All that dumb shit you used to own when things were good is now gone. Cleaned out of the condo and emptied from the $800 a month heated parking space. And that's when it happens. When it's already too late. When you finally come to realize that "action" is indeed a dirty word.

It took me a little a while to figure out why Brian always referred to his people as *our friends in Wilmington.* Wilmington, Delaware was where all the credit card companies relocated back in the 1980s, so they could take advantage of Delaware's obscure free market laws and screw the public on predatory interest rates.

Yup, loansharking.

2010 was the year of the *vig*. The Wall Street boys were out of work and trying to play poker for a living. *I could relate.* But you see, Wall Street guys like to think they're good at poker because they deal with things like "risk" and "equity" and "zero sum games." It was like they all forgot why they lost their fucking jobs in the first place. Most of these guys are massive net losers, and a lot of them were hell-bent on putting their severance bonuses to work after they'd helped their masters offload your grandparents' pensions and 401ks.

And so, little Wilmington was born, right down here in Hell's Kitchen. It was time to get ours.

On more than one occasion, I got a good look at the game sheet and saw how much money was actually going out of that place. I estimated that Brian and Wilmington were making about twenty large a week on the vig alone. The only reason they set up the card games in the first place was to chum the waters for the much more lucrative loansharking operation. The game was a machine that produced gambling debt. With a $50 rake, no one could beat it, so even the best players were losing over the long haul. Then, eventually, they have a couple bad weeks and have to go "on the sheet"—that means borrowing money to get back into the game. Then, of course, they lose that too and have to pay twenty points a week until they're caught up—which also almost never happens. This adds up to an unholy amount of profit for Brian and Wilmington.

Yeah, it didn't take long for me to figure out that I was a proxy for crimes that were far worse than what I was employed to do. My position was created to insulate the people in charge from the actual day-to-day legwork that was required to find the potential debtors, and then bust them. If the game ever got popped, Brian and

Wilmington would be watching it all on camera from a remote location. Shit, maybe in *Wilmington, Delaware* for all I knew. I didn't know much. KGB and I were middle management: the everyday grease monkeys tasked with keeping the machine running at all times. We had no connection to the serious money.

The level of planning that went into this whole operation was some seriously conspiratorial shit, and it made me wonder just how high-profile and *organized* these "friends in Wilmington" really were.

It also made me wonder about some of these poor-bastard players who I knew were getting in way too deep, had lost everything and more, and then eventually stopped showing up. *Like Jiwoo. Where the fuck was he? Did he stop playing because of a parental ultimatum? Or did he move back to Korea for fear of who he owed? Or was he just plain GONE?* Brian told me that his scare tactics were all bullshit, but part of me wondered if he was only showing me the collection methods that he wanted me to know about. I'd seen a lot of other poor bastards disappear since then. *Like Barry. What the fuck happened to Barry? You never met Barry. A good guy, but bad with money. Anyway, now Barry's gone too.* I guess I hoped I would never have to find out what happened to him. It was way too late to turn back. I was already making too much fucking money.

9

So I'm sitting at the cage, which is right near the main security door, playing some kind of stupid bird game on my phone, when suddenly there's a bang at the door so loud and heavy it feels like an explosion.

A pressure wave bumps me in the guts, and adrenaline is instantly dumped into my blood. Everyone at the table jumps all at once, then looks over toward the door, then at Matt and me. They all have the same look on their face: like someone's just invaded their anuses. Apparently, Matt's the only one who knows exactly what's going on right now, because he runs over to the cage and grabs the house phone, throws it into the sink, and turns on the faucet. He then runs over to the cash box, finds the player with the deepest stack, and throws about five grand at him—looks him dead in the eye and points his finger accusingly, "You were *paid*." After that, Matt tears the game sheet out of the book and stuffs it down the back of his pants. He does all of this in under fifteen seconds.

There's another bang at the door, even louder than the last one, and this time the bottom comes pushing out about six inches before snapping back into place. The magnetic jamb lock won't give, but whoever's behind there isn't giving up. This time, someone from behind the door yells, "Police! We have a warrant!" But the fact that they didn't yell "police" the first time makes me feel even worse about what I think is going to happen.

Whoever's behind there is still wailing away, and I look over at Harris who quickly jumps up out of the box and moves to an empty seat at the table—like it's fucking musical chairs. He looks relieved now that he's seated at the table and not in the dealer chair—like this might actually save his ass. Maybe it will. I have no idea.

They're still wailing away on the door, but it simply won't give. That jamb lock is really on there. Brian had this place retrofitted like a vault—*like a place where all the money is.* Theses fuckers might actually have to kill the power to get in. It's clear to me that Matt has been in this kind of situation before, so I just stand out of his way and let him do what he thinks is best. After pausing a second to think, he comes back over to the cage and looks into the security monitor. His expression reads like he's trying to verify something. He looks back at me gravely and says, "Alright, just take it easy. Don't say shit to these motherfuckers. We have lawyer. He's Jew." I look him deep in the eye and nod as though I understand completely. Then, Matt picks up the remote that unlocks the door, and he looks back at me one more time. He takes in a deep breath like we're on a space shuttle and he's about to open the airlock. He smiles at me and says in that thick, gloomy-ass Russian accent of his, "I hope you brought your ass plug today, buddy. We're going to the *Tombs*." Then he presses down on the button that opens the security door.

Matt and I throw our hands in the air as fifteen SWAT-looking motherfuckers come filing into the room. This is not the way I'd always pictured it. I thought it'd be more like old-school detectives in shitty Men's Wearhouse suits, black patent leather, service revolvers, three-day beards, and the lingering musk of booze and cheap tobacco. No, this is a post-9/11 raid: Blackwater-looking douchebags in full body armor, submachines guns with fucking flashlights on the ends, riot masks—one of these assholes has an e-cig tucked into the loop of his Kevlar. I think I smell Axe Body Spray.

Every one of us, including every player in the room, now has a sub-machinegun pointed at their head or chest. There are more cops than people in this room. Chris-the-ambulance-chaser—some idiot, jerkoff lawyer who I fucking hate—starts immediately freaking out about how he's going to get disbarred if he's caught in here. He starts screaming and pleading to one of the cops, "You gotta help me, bro. You gotta let me go! I can't be *seen* in here, man! People know me! You gotta let me outta here!" He starts to stand up, nervously wiping his hands through his long hair like the total coke fiend that he is, and a couple of the cops start yelling at him to "Sit the fuck down! Don't fucking move!" But it just makes everything worse, and he starts to stand up again, this time more insistent, and he actually REACHES for one of the cops, "You gotta help me, BRO!" Two of the cops immediately mace his ass, and another comes over and chops his gut with the butt of his bull-pup rifle. I accidentally blurt out a nervous laugh as they cave in Chris-the-Ambulance-Chaser's solar plexus. I knew he would be the one to bitch out like this. Then the sergeant, or whoever the fuck, comes over and gets right up in my face, "You think that's funny, shitbird?" I immediately straighten up and say, "No, *sir*." Matt just rolls his eyes at me.

Three of the cops dissemble from the group and toss the place looking for drugs, guns, and money—anything they can pin on us to make the charges worse. They locate the rest of the cash and confiscate it as "evidence." They find a baggie of weed on the floor under the table. It clearly belongs to one of the nit-bastard players, but none of them take responsibility for it.

"Hey *Vor!*" A short, Hitler-mustached cop addresses Matt as he brings over the eighth of weed and presents it to him. "What do we have here? Runnin' a little more than just cards in this place, are ya?"

Matt looks the cop dead in the eye, then down at the bag of weed in his black Kevlar glove. "Looks like the same shit that killed Bruce Lee. I wouldn't touch it." So, they of course pin it on Matt because he's the only minority/immigrant among us, but he doesn't say shit about it. Just looks straight ahead and takes it like a man. Like a straight-up Russian man.

They turn the place upside down, trashing everything. They cut the felt from the table with a box-cutter. They bag up the chips and money (which they'll *unbag* and steal later). Searching for more contraband, they toss the contents of the cupboard, turn the cage over, rip apart the couch, and empty the wastebasket and refrigerator onto the kitchen floor. They find nothing of course. They steal all the beer in the closet, dismount the sixty-inch flat-screen from the wall, and steal that too. The commanding officer looks at Matt, gives him a shit-eating grin and says, "Evidence." I'm starting to think that Matt and this asshole share a history.

Then we watch them line up all of the players against the wall and ask them one-by-one, "Who's house? Who's house? Okay, asshole, who's the house here?" They all point to me, Matt, and Harris with the same sorry look of shame on their faces. I can't blame them; no one's about to say "fuck the po-lice" after what they just did to Chris-the-Ambulance-Chaser.

After every one of the players rats us the fuck out, they let each one go, then escort us out of the apartment in cuffs. The entire process takes over two hours. *Fucking overtime.* As I walk down the hall with an officer holding the back of my arm, there's this hot little blonde number coming out of her apartment in her tight little workout clothes. She looks at all of us with wide, shocked eyes. I pass by her with my hands cuffed behind my back, and I wink at her like, *Yeah, right under your nose, baby. Right in your home.*

As we exit the building in police custody, I see Chris-the-Ambulance-Chaser sitting there on the back of an *actual* ambulance, taking a police report with an oxygen mask over his face, his hand resting protectively over his gut as a paramedic takes his vitals. He looks back at me with no discerning expression as we board the paddy wagon, and his stupid fucking face is the last thing I see as they slam the rear doors closed.

It's going to be a long night.

Manhattan Central Booking. 100 Centre Street

Two Stars on Yelp.

Direct from the sally gate it's typically three hours to

get transferred from NYPD to DOC—take our mugs, ask if we're dope-sick by the Fire Department's medical personnel, empty our pockets, relinquish our shoelaces and belts, get our papers. Then they stick us way down there in "The Tombs," this massive shitty bullpen with an open toilet area, so if you have to shit, you have to do it in front of everybody.

And now we wait.

They put me and KGB in the same cell. I have no idea what happened to Harris. Maybe priors or a warrant. Maybe he told them he was dope-sick, which might have been the smart thing, since you get to wait in the hospital with a clean bed and a nice fat dose of Suboxone, instead of down here with the cold steel, grimy concrete, and government cheese. Matt informs me that he has the phone number of our lawyer sewn into the waistband of his underpants, so as soon as it's our turn to use the phone we should be out of here in less than twenty hours. If it weren't for Matt, I'm pretty sure I'd be fucked right now.

It's a weeknight, Matt informs me, so it's not mobbed the way it would be on a weekend. A few sad-looking souls look so harmless it's hard to picture them doing anything that might land them in this place. No obvious gang bangers. Not even an Occupy protestor. Just me, Matt, and a few soft saggy bums, burnouts, and one half-alive middle-aged tranny. For hours, we sit and wait.

Matt sighs. "Fuck man, three times in two years. I don't know, maybe it's time to retire."

"What would you do instead?"

"Well, I have this idea for a *app*."

"Yeah? What kind of app?"

"It's a *app* where, anybody who has the *app*, can get a new kitten, *every* month."

"Did you say a new *kitten*?"

"Yes. *Every* month."

"What, like a *cat share*?"

"Yes. But we *only* do kittens—because, you know, cat really sucks after it's done being kitten. So you get kitten for thirty to ninety days, then someone comes and picks it up. Then *boom*, another new kitten. Then thirty days later, *boom*, same thing, another kitten. So long as you pay, it never stops."

"Interesting. You get the novelty of a new pet every thirty days, with none of the responsibility."

"Exactly. But we *only* do kittens."

"That's ingenious."

"Thanks, buddy."

"But what do you do with the old kittens?"

"What do you mean? You get a new one, *every* month. Then it goes to someone else who has the *app*."

"Right, but what happens to the kittens after they become cats, and no one wants them anymore? What do you do with all those grown-ass cats?"

"Listen … it's not important … you get *new* kitten …*every* month—"

"Right, but—"

"The point is you don't have to worry about it. That's the service. You let us *app* people worry about it. What happens to the cats once they get old, that's no one's concern but ours."

"I see."

Matt stands up, stretches a little and sighs longingly. "Or … maybe I start up a pet *removal* service. That one is probably easier. You don't need to make a *app* for that one. Apps are *expensive*, bro."

The C.O.s keep moving us through a series of bullpens of varying sizes, what Matt tells me is one step closer to court, and most probably, freedom. At some point, we get to the pen with the phones. Matt does his thing, calls our lawyer, or maybe calls Brian who calls our lawyer. The C.O.s call us by name a few times. I do exactly what Matt does. After a series of even shittier cells, a white, head-shaved C.O., with full-sleeve tats, puts me in my own cell a couple of times, and puts all the minorities, including Matt, in the tighter shittier pens with one another. Fifteen more hours of this shit and we finally get up to court where Josh our lawyer is bag-eyed and waiting for us.

I felt a little weird immediately after the raid. Brian wasn't around. He wasn't even in the country when it happened, and I was the one who was supposed to be holding shit down for a few weeks while he was away in Panama on some kind of "money laundering vacation" or whatever-the-fuck. He didn't call me back for over a week. Finally, I received a collect call after I guess Wilmington finally got around to checking the security cameras. They never even tried reaching out to me—paranoid twerps. The protocol was that Brian was always the only point of contact, no matter what. If Brian ever disappeared there would be no one to answer to. It was over.

When I told him what happened he said, "*Shit!* Was anyone sent away? You know, like, *permanently*?"

"No, not really," I told him. "They just locked us all up for the night, and your boy Josh got us out in the morning."

"Okay, good. Did any of the cops ask about me? Did anyone mention my name?"

"Not that I know of. Matt and I were together for most of it, but they took Harris somewhere else since he told them he was dope sick."

"Ha-ha! Sneaky fucker. Probably had a nice bed and some Jell-O while you guys were down there freezing your dicks off."

"Yeah, well, they just locked us up, processed us, and let us go, pretty much."

"Okay, good. Sounds like a standard, run-of-the-mill raid then. So how are things going right now?"

"Uh … What do you mean?"

"How's the game? I assume it's a little weaker now, considering."

"No … I mean … I haven't been over there."

"*What? Why?* Why the fuck haven't you been over there?"

"Pardon?"

"Why isn't the game running right now? How long has it been since you've been over there?"

"I don't know, about … two weeks, I guess?"

"Two *weeks*! Fucking *Jesus*! *Why?* Have you tried since then?"

"I mean … the cops broke in and put guns in everyone's faces and trashed the place, Brian. I just assumed—"

"Assumed what? That we *close down* because we got popped one time?"

"Well, we all got arrested, man. I dunno—"

"Yeah, that's typically what happens in a *raid*, bro. But if no one was hurt and no one went away, or was even *interrogated*, then why are you not trying to get games off again?"

"Well, I … I dunno."

"Listen. This is a *business*, bro. This is what we DO. It comes with the territory. Sometimes you get fucked. *When* that happens, you pick up and get on with it. How much did we lose?"

"Like, ten."

"Ten? That's it? So, ten grand and no one went away? That's pretty fucking amazing, man. That's actually a fucking *record* min loss."

Brian gives me a chance to speak, but I got nothing.

"Listen to me, bro. This is *New York*. The police arrest ordinary everyday citizens all the time. They do it for smoking in the public, for not having a goddamn bell on their bicycle, for just getting into a good old-fashioned bar fight. Almost everyone who's been here for more than a decade has been arrested for some stupid bullshit, at least once. It's not a big deal, man."

"I see."

"Look, we're going to need you to reopen as soon as possible. Dump everyone from the list who was there that night, and get everything back on track. I'll see you in a couple weeks. You should be open again in no less than *FIVE* business days. *Capiche?*"

"Yeah, okay."

"Did anyone from Wilmington try and contact you?"

"No. I mean, I don't think so. The cops took our phones. But no one's been by my place or anything. Why?"

Brian pauses a moment, and there's this sort of eerie dead silence for what seems like way too long.

"Hello?"

"Yeah … No … It's … It's fine. I'll deal with it when I get back. Don't worry about it."

"Alright … I'll try and get things up and running again as soon as possible."

"My man. *Listen*, don't sweat this. This is just what happens sometimes. We're fucking *New Yorkers*, bro. After Giuliani, this whole place is like a … fucking … Orwellian shopping mall or some shit. People go to jail here. It's nothing personal. It doesn't *mean* anything. So, if no one goes away for real, when we get out, we move on, right?"

"Right, okay."

"All right. Good luck. I'll see you when I get back."

And then he hangs up the phone.

We reopened the Midtown game in a brand-new location less than three weeks after we were raided. We thought we'd accurately deduced where we'd fucked up, after having read the police report, which stated that they'd had an "undercover officer" at the game to confirm that the activities were indeed illegal. It wasn't hard to figure out who the cop was; it was that asshole who looked like a fucking cop. So the new security and prevention protocol was simple: *Don't let anyone who looks like a cop into the poker game. When screening new players, have them text you a picture of their work ID, a business card, and their driver's license; then, check their fucking Facebook; if all their friends have mustaches and there's a lot of Budweiser at the BBQ pics, then tell them the game is closed. Or tell them to fuck off. If someone seems weird, just pass. Don't do dumb shit, and we'll all continue to earn a soft and easy living.*

But when they raided us again less than six months after we reopened, we didn't know what to think. The second raid, the cops weren't as nice. When Harris tried locking himself in the bathroom to flush all of his drugs, they dragged him out by his neck and laid into him so everyone could see. The cuffs were tighter this time, the interrogation closer to our faces, the threats more personal. They told KGB they were going to send his ass back to Russia. And me, they bitch-slapped with a plastic-reinforced Kevlar glove once they'd discovered that I had taken all the cash, balled it up into fistfuls, and sent it sailing off of the balcony, right out onto Sixth Avenue during rush hour traffic.

This time, I had less than a minute when they started whaling away on the door. I decided to turn the situation into an opportunity to disappoint the NYPD. This turned out to be a mistake. The people on the streets went apeshit—hungrily grabbing handfuls of exploding cash balls all over Avenue of the Americas, greedily looking up into the sky as if somehow expecting more. One man even caused a small accident after running out in front of an oncoming taxi as he chased a few twenties that were blowing down the street. After slapping the shit out of me, NYPD slapped me with "intent to incite a riot." But my real *intent* was simply to make sure that the money went to anyone but the fucking pigs. *No "evidence" for you, cocksuckers.*

But despite my exercise in civil disobedience, I got off light again. The judge didn't even seem to give a shit that I was back within six months and for the exact same offense. He didn't even look down at me during the proceeding. Just a cursory glance through my sheet and a quick, barely punitive decision. I was kind of offended by his indifference. Like, *if you don't actually give a shit, then why not just leave us the fuck alone?* But this time the charge was going to stick and they made me give the government my DNA since I was now a repeat offender. I went in and they stuck these little wooden sticks into my month, scraped the insides of my cheeks, bagged it up and sent it off to God knows where. Now they had all the biological markers they'd need to track me for life. This was indeed some serious Orwellian shit, and all because I ran a poker game in the living room of *someone's* apartment.

When we all got out for the second time and tried making

sense of where we went wrong, the new police report stated that a "police informant" had been present to confirm illegal activities. When we asked Josh-the-lawyer about this, he told us that an informant could be literally anyone. It appeared that now the pigs were pulling down-and-out d-gens off the streets and giving them three hundred bucks to go free-roll city games in exchange for information. This time we had no idea who it was that ratted us because it could have been anyone we didn't know personally, which was basically everyone. This made for a lot of uncertainty when faced with the decision to move forward.

But word down the Wilmington pipeline was that we would continue. Business as usual. No one, including Brian, seemed concerned or to notice that the heat was now officially *on*. To them, it was like nothing ever happened. There was no meeting. There were no memos or revised protocols. The word was: "Please be ready to reopen for business in two weeks or less. K. Thx. Bye."

It was then that I realized I had no control over anything that was going on in that place. I was their bitch, plain and simple, and theirs was an operation whose dealings had little need or regard for me as its formal daily operator. I was a shill, a peon, a half-assed fall guy. This *thing of theirs*, or whatever the fuck it was, was controlled by dangerous people who took serious risks and who were clearly under constant pressure to keep it moving forward at all costs. It was organized. It had fucking shareholders. *Wilmington Incorporated.* They weren't going anywhere.

On the morning I got out of jail again, I decided to go for a walk. It wasn't exactly a pleasant walk, as most aren't during the midmorning rush, but it was still an exercise of freedom, which I felt was vaguely important at the time. I headed uptown. I was tired but I wasn't ready to head all the way back to my apartment in Brooklyn. I wasn't ready for all the yahoos on the subway, assholes singing, yelling, and jacking off in public. I had spent yet another thirty hours locked in a steel cage, dealing with the same shit, and the idea of a subway car seemed like another jail cell to me at the time. All I wanted to do was walk in a straight line for a little while. Then maybe I'd go back home with a bottle of whiskey and some dinner. Y*eah, the liquor store. Always the savior.*

But as I walked on by, trying to avoid just about everything society had to offer, I was stopped by a vision.

On the corner, opposite me, stood a poor, little old lady with an even older, shittier-looking dog. The two of them looked tired, worn, and peeled back. Ready for the end.

They were standing there together, waiting at the crosswalk for the light to signal—just standing and waiting.

Finally, the light signaled, and the two of them drearily trudged onward towards the other side of the street. As they approached the center of Sixth Avenue, the old dog stopped, planted himself, and started shitting right there in the middle of the road. The old lady tried pulling at the dog's leash, but he wouldn't budge. They had a few seconds before the oncoming traffic at the light ahead of them would surge forward, and at first the old woman just laughed nervously, "Oh, come on Rufus, not here." But the dog wouldn't budge. After a few more seconds, and it becoming more apparent that they might not make it in time, panic gripped the old woman. She started screaming and pleading with the old bastard, tugging at his leash with intense frantic jerks. But the dog was taking his time with this one. He was old and uncomfortable and he needed to shit. He didn't care anymore about love or loyalty or obedience, or whether he might get a fucking treat later. He just wanted some goddamned *relief.* And so, he dug in and held fast, right in the middle of a four-lane avenue.

The light went from red to green, and the cars started coming. They didn't stop. They came forward, *ever* forward, indifferent and unsmiling. They didn't slow down. They sped up! But the dog held his ground. He was finally taking a stand, the only way he knew how, right there in the middle of oncoming traffic. The cars zipped past the old woman and her dog, honking, stopping short, skidding and screeching everywhere, their engines revving. The woman broke down and fell to her knees as more and more vehicles angrily honked and sped by. I found myself, standing there on the corner, frozen with empathic dread. All I could do was watch. I couldn't speak. I couldn't even move. *And then the son of a bitch looked right up at me! Right in my fucking eye.* My heart sank, and my stomach knotted. I stared back into the dog's eyes and held his gaze, as he continued squatting and shaking there in the center of the street. And for a split second, for the first time in my life, I could truly feel another creature's deep, *deep* sorrow, anxiety, and hopelessness. There was some kind of cosmic truth floating there between us—a kind of knowing that only weird-ass beings like ourselves truly shared. The dog and I *knew it.* We were trapped in a world overrun by cretins. By *people.* People who owned massive, expensive, deadly machines, and who would whizz by us forever, cruel and uncaring. Fucking *People.* People who wouldn't even stop for a helpless old lady, much less a helpless old dog, because they were all in a hurry and needed to get to the goddamn Starbucks and the fuckin' Dunkin Donuts.

10

Find somebody.

This is what people do, yes? When they're lonely and damaged and empty inside—they *find someone.* Someone to fill it all up. Someone to argue with over dinner, in public. Someone to shop with on Saturdays. Someone to watch television with three hours before bedtime every night after the vapid exchanges at their socially damaging jobs. Misery adores company, especially if you get to have sex with it on occasion.

Since moving to "the city," I'd seen a lot of dudes who were a hell of a lot fatter and uglier than I was walking around town with good-looking women on their arm. *Arm candy.* So many software nerds and boring, dull finance jerkoffs and lawyers, just walking around casually, abusing the shit out of the girls they never got to fuck during their formative years when it really mattered. The common denominator seemed to be *money*, which I now had plenty of. And here I was, now two years in, residing in the city with the world's greatest collection of fit, easy women and nothing to show for it. How had I let life slip by me so easily and for so long? How was I not on top of this shit?

And so, I decided one day, when, after having a significant piece of my soul sucked out by New York's poker community, that I too would find someone attractive to have sex with. I already knew from my experience in the world, that the best place to find the worst kind of woman was of course at the bar, so that's the first place I went looking. This was an entirely conscious decision. A quest for damage. Something so distracting, that in the context of my current living hell, couldn't possibly make my work life any worse by comparison.

I left Manhattan for Brooklyn, hoping for an easier score with the lessers. The demographic I was in search of consisted of a meth-addict-nympho with really toned legs, tits optional, and who might also get violently repellent after all physical demands were met. I knew she was in Brooklyn somewhere. She had to be.

So, I find some shithole in Bushwick, and it's the kind of place that's trying to be a shithole, but it has some of the indiest whiskies and craft brews around, so I guess this is a good place to start. The joint is basically empty, save for a few permanently embalmed middle-aged freaks and one younger rakish-looking Asian woman at the other end of the bar.

I think she's Japanese, and I think she might also be a chubby chaser because I just caught her checking out the supple rolls of butterfat scrunch up inside my black t-shirt as I bellied up to the bar. *I caught her!* At this point in my life, I'm self-aware enough to know that I basically resemble a large muscular house cat, baby-faced with youthful skin, big and bearded and soft around the edges. And, I also know, from my being a man of the world, that this is basically what every Japanese girl has been conditioned to want since birth: a big beautiful *cat man*, thick and warm and marbled with butterfat.

She's been making eyes at me for the past few minutes, and she's drinking over there all alone. Don't get me wrong, I can already tell by the shape of her that I'd fuck the bejesus out of her in a heartbeat, but her lack of subtlety is really spooking me right now. I haven't even had my first yet, nor a minute to sit down and relax, and already I see her walking towards me. When things are this instant, the paranoid wires start buzzing and the noradrenaline gets dumped—*that feeling you get when you know you shouldn't be somewhere.* But this is what I came for, so I decide not to bitch out and sprint for the door, which is my instinctive immediate reaction. Instead, I decide to wait and see. *Let her in.*

She takes the stool nearest me and leans into the bar, pretending like this might be a better place to get the bartender's attention. And as she does this, she gets weirdly close to me, and then I feel her arm press into mine. This means nothing to me at first, but when she doesn't move it away, while continuing to wait there, I start to get really uncomfortable. Clearly, she knows that her arm is pressing up against mine. I can feel it, which means she can feel it. That's how it works. But why is she doing this? What does she expect me to do? Am I supposed to move it? Am I supposed to say something about it? *Excuse me, Miss, I couldn't help but notice you're touching my fucking arm. Would you like to have sex in the bathroom?* I don't know the correct response to this kind of situation, which I assume is rare, so I continue to sit there, with her arm still pressed up against mine, as I stare straight ahead and try to pretend like none of this is happening.

The problem here, however, is that she has to know I'm pretending because she knows that I know her arm is touching mine, so now it's obvious to the both of us that I've already fucked up this situation beyond repair. To make things even worse, she then slowly turns her head a full ninety degrees to look at me, all of which I can completely make out in my periphery, but I'm still too paralyzed with fear to turn and face her. But even if I could, what then? Stare back? What would or could I possibly say that might fix any of this, after she's already gone and done something like put her arm up against me and stare at the side of my fucking head? So, I just continue to sit there facing the bar, unblinking, catatonic, my eyebrows probably somewhat raised in alertness, as I now pretend that I can't see this woman's staring face from less than fifteen inches away.

As the tension mounts beyond conception I feel like I might actually burst into tears because of it. *No!* I tell myself, *DO NOT do that. That really is the worst possible thing. Where the fuck is this cocksucking bartender?* I desperately need someone to come save me from all of this. Or maybe just one goddamn drink would help. But this lazy hipster bastard bartender is nowhere to be found. After another full minute passes—the perceptive time-equivalent of holding one's hand over an open flame—this asshole broke-dick Johnny-Depp-look-alike-motherfucker finally comes over to take her fucking order. He ignores me of course.

After he makes her drinks and walks away without acknowledging me, she starts nudging me with her arm. It's now obvious she's trying to get my attention, so now I have no choice but to look over at her. I turn my head to her, slowly—too slow, in fact—my eyes huge and alert, and she makes big eyes back at me, mocking the way I must look. She says "Hi?" like *Hi, dipshit.*

As she exhales the word "hi," I can smell her breath,

and it's all bready like fresh pancake batter mixed with top-shelf whiskey. There's a sudden, violent biochemical reaction inside me that sends blood swirling in my groin. *If I get a hard on now, I'm going to kill myself in the bathroom.* I can see now that she is in fact very attractive, which makes this situation even harder for me to deal with. I'm half-hoping to Christ she has some kind of weird defect—like a prosthetic leg or one single obvious tit, or one of those fingerless little midget arms with the single little nail on the end—just anything that'll allow me some emotional control over this situation.

"Hi," I say back, barely able to hold eye contact, and then she slides a double of some kind of whiskey at me. I look down and say "Oh, thanks … What is it?"

"Willet," she says, like I'm supposed to know what the fuck *willet* is, so I say "Oh," like a complete tool, and then a perky "Thank you!"

This is a total power move on her part, buying me a drink without even saying hello first. It's half turning me on and half making a bitch out of me. She's really owning this situation right now, and there's nothing I can think to do to turn it around at this point. I'm hers to do whatever she wants with.

In situations like these, I have to ask, "Why me?" When an attractive, rare, and exotic creature starts coming on with spooky sexual attention, these are the kinds of things that make me nervous—that make me feel like I might wake up in the morning with one less kidney. I came into this place looking for six-and-halves and a little damage, and now there's a Japanese fertility goddess buying me drinks and making the kind of advances that should scream "black widow" to any man who's ever been in a set up situation, which, come to think of it, has basically been my entire existence over the past decade.

She looks over at me and gives me this look like, "say something correct now."

So, as calmly as I can, I say the words, "So … What nationality are you?"

WRONG.

"Japanese," she says, coldly. "*Obviously.*"

"Yes, *obviously*," I say. "I'm sorry."

She raises one eyebrow, giving me a look like I just failed her and that she has no choice but to kill me now.

"So," she says, "What do you do?" She already sounds bored as she sighs and rolls her eyes.

In a moment of impulse I decide to just tell her the truth. Not because I'm an honest person, but because I'm not relaxed enough to lie. "I move money around for people," I tell her, as I take a nervous sip from my drink.

"Really?" she says, suddenly interested. "Like money *laundering*? That's cool."

"Not exactly," I tell her, and then she instantly looks down, disappointed and bored again. I nervously backpedal, try and rework this image she prefers. "Well, something *like* that. Not exactly money laundering. But *illegal* for sure … in Manhattan," I tell her, pointing with my thumb over my shoulder for some reason—like Manhattan is definitely back that way—though I actually have no idea which direction I'm facing.

She starts laughing at me, "Why?" she says, between laughs, like I'm clearly not the type, and I clearly have other options.

"It's a long story," I tell her.

As we head outside for a cigarette—because even in the filthiest, grittiest bar in Bushwick you're not allowed to smoke—she goes first and I follow her, looking down like I do. You can tell by the angles of her that she was one of those girls who spent her entire childhood priming adolescent development for a perfect body with ballet and gymnastics and raw nutritious meals. Born in a land of discipline and honor and ruthless uncompromising work ethic, years of hard endurance and incessant strenuous activity sculpting perfect legs and ass, while I was back in Middle America playing Nintendo on a couch six hours every day, eating Fudge Rounds and drinking pop between naps and mindless television. And now here we are: an out of shape, dumb-ass white man with an attractive, fierce Japanese woman drinking top-shelf liquor in New York City. Tell me life is fair.

After smoking in silence for several minutes, she comes at me close, grabs my arm, and pulls me into her, so she can whisper in my ear: "I want to see your casino."

Lately, we've been rotating two Midtown games between Eastside and Westside locations in an effort to cut down on the foot traffic in each building. One half of the week we're in Hell's Kitchen, the other half we're in Murray Hill. This way, the joyless fucks who live on the Upper West Side and the post-frat-boy Wall Street cocksuckers who live in Murray Hill both have convenient access to gambling one half of every week. It's expensive, having two locations, but anything we can do to reliably quell suspicion among nosey bastard neighbors and switch it up on the NYPD snitches is well worth it. Tonight is a Murray Hill night, so the Westside game is closed. She and I take a cab from Bushwick to Hell's Kitchen.

I know there's a fridge full of beer over there, and I keep reminding myself that there's no reasonable or *chivalrous* way to fuck her in a vacant card room, so I try to eliminate the thought from my head, but it's hard with that little skirt she has on and the way she keeps rubbing those folded calves together—it's all forcing the scheming side of my brain to get more and more involved.

As we enter the building I say hello to Mike-the-doorman. This is the first time he's actually looked at me suspiciously. He knows my usual presence here is vaguely "business-related," but we slip him a c-note often enough so that he doesn't ask. I walk by with her, and he gives me a look like, *Ooh,* Japanese? *Nice!*

I decide to take her to the rooftop first because there's a really good view up there. I have no idea if she even gives a shit. We step into the elevator and without warning she procures a bottle of indie rye from her enormous bag. She pops it open, takes the first pull, and then shoves the bottle into my chest.

"Here, *drink* this," she tells me.

"Fine," I say.

When we get up to the roof she doesn't seem at all impressed. We step to the edge and look out into all that speckled light—the glowing windows of skyscraping corporations, the new identical unfinished condo developments all over Midtown.

"Do you *like* it here?" I ask her.

She says nothing at first, takes another drink from the bottle, and stares blankly back the other way, out towards New Jersey.

"When I first came here I felt very lonely," she tells me. "After years of watching how people behave in this place, I think this city is probably not good for people. It makes them feel important, which is not a good thing. But I've been here a long time. I don't really think about it anymore."

"Why did you leave Japan?" I ask her.

She sighs and takes another pull from the bottle. "School," she says, rolling her eyes, "Video animation," she adds in a mocking tone, as if video animation is the dumbest thing ever. "And so now I'm head waitress at fucking Sushi *Samba.*"

She moves back away from me and leans over the building's edge, looking down onto the street from several hundred feet above.

"There are worse things," I tell her.

She shoots me a look, her eyes squinted tight like she can barely stand the sight of me. "*Obviously,*" she says as she eyes me up and down.

She pushes the bottle back at my chest and sits me down on one of the plastic deck chairs, then climbs on top of me, straddling my lap. I look down, and I can see *everything* peeking out from under that short little skirt.

She moves in close to my face, orbits my head from ear-to-ear, the strands of her thick black hair electrifying my nerves as it lightly brushes around my face. It smells different to me than other girls' hair. Not like that artificial fruit-and-flower scent you expect from an American girl—that Bath & Body Works shit. This is something different. Something natural. Something exotic. Something good.

"You know, when I first came here, I needed money for school, so I studied how to become dominatrix."

"That's interesting," I tell her.

"I think it's time to go downstairs to your casino now," she tells me, as she pulls at my belt buckle and breathes on my neck.

"Um …" I push back a little in the chair and look at her. "It's not really set up for that sort of thing," I tell her. "No one really *lives* down there, you know?" Which isn't exactly true. I lived down there for over a year.

She looks at me incredulously and says, "But isn't there a *really big table* down there?"

11

It's 4 p.m., and I've just woken up. I put on some day-old clothing and hit the streets because I want to be outside before the sun goes down. As I get off the subway I walk right past Earth Waffle on 42nd Street, and I glide euphorically, almost weightless, into the Liquor Emporium. As I look at all that liquor, all lined up there and ready to go, my mouth waters a little, and I'm smiling for the first time in maybe weeks. I'm in a good mood because it's Rosh Hashanah, and half of New York went back to New Jersey for the holiday. I have two full days off, so tonight she and I are having a "drugs and sex night" at her place (her words, not mine). Between the two of us, she's the one with the better apartment, and every one of her five Jewish roommates is out of town for the holiday. This is going to be a real treat. *Sex. In private. In a home. On someone else's bed.*

I'm walking down the street singing the Rosh Hashanah song in my head:

Rosh ha sha nah …
Rosh ha sha nah …
Hey hey hey …
Go-od bye …
I'm a great mood.

She has given me a list of several things that I need to accomplish before I meet with her this evening: I'm to procure one gram of MDMA; one eight ball of cocaine; something strong, clean, and voluminous to drink; one Viagra or Cialis (my call). And some lube.

So far I've got the big strong booze in my hand and I'm all ready to cash out, but there's this middle-aged, blue-blooded hag in front of me (a true New Yorker), and she's holding up the line because she's not yet finished admonishing the minority slave behind the counter for refusing to open the second register for her. All of this, mind you, occurs *after* she's completed her transaction.

The poor bastard offers her some lame excuse— something about the register being closed because all of the receipts have been counted for the shift and blah blah blah. But *Madam Bigtime* won't let up on the poor son of a bitch. She keeps laying into him with accusations of laziness, poor work ethic, and the unwillingness to pull himself up by his "bootstraps." *Jesus.*

"Listen to me, young man. You should be able to do the math at the second register *via* long hand in case business is *booming*. Someday the CEO of a *major* company will walk in here, and he'll be *watching*. If you had the wherewithal and the *initiative* to do the *right* thing, a man of that caliber would be wholly impressed by your ability and motivation to go the extra mile. Someone like that could *change your life*! That is how things *happen* in America, you know."

The kid just glares at her like, *Bitch, in my country you'd be raped and murdered on the side of a dirt road.*

She goes on: "I'm *serious*, young man. This is how people meet opportunity here. You'd do well to go out of your way to impress the kind of people who have the power to *change your life*."

The woman struts out of the liquor store with her cheap white wine and her nose pointed upward. I look at the kid sympathetically as I put a handle of Bulleit down on the counter. "Don't worry, man. None of what that bitch said was true."

He replies with a half-hearted, "I know," and looks at the ground, defeated. I can tell he really does know. He's been here long enough to know the truth; no one here is going to help him; no one here is going to give him an opportunity. He's on his own, like everybody else.

My druggist is a Hispanic homosexual named Moises. He drives a Lexus—a *nice one*. Moises does all of his business out of his car. He rolls through the city like an Uber driver and waits for calls. He comes to you, you get in, he drives you a few blocks while his little brother in the backseat weighs out your shit, then he drops you off wherever you want to go (so long as it's in Manhattan below 110th Street). It's a great service, and they have everything you need. And I mean *everything*: dust, amyls, blow, hydro, hash, the *good* acid (like the shit they had back in the sixties that didn't kill you), and all the big pharma-grade shit, like the hard-on pills I'm supposed to get today. He even gets his hands on the old-school Quaaludes. Moises keeps his ride and his whole operation nice and *tight*. He is, by all definitions, a successful American businessman, and I have great respect for him.

Moises is a sick maniac gambler too. That's how I discovered him. He used to play in our game about a year back, but now that he's a fucking millionaire he plays in a much bigger game uptown where it's all drug money. I'm not allowed into that game. Believe me, I've asked. *No civilians, esé.*

Anyway, Moises picks me up on the corner of 43rd and Ninth, and begins circling the block. His little brother, Javier, sits low in the backseat with the attaché briefcase full of serious jail-time.

"Hey Timmy *boi*, what'jew need, Papi?" Moises is not wearing a shirt today for some reason. The AC is full blast. I assume it's to keep him from sweating into the car's fine leather. The air is all *new car smell* and whatever expensive cologne he's got on—I wouldn't know. He's wearing his big dumb Armani goggle shades today, too. I give him my list and my money. "Dayum, son! You gettin' your Chorizo wrapped tonight?"

"God willing," I tell him.

"I's you bro, I'd leave God out of this one. This some Devil-worship shit you got goin' on right here. None of my business though—"

"You're right about that."

"—Javier!" Moises barks over his shoulder towards the backseat. "Hook my boy up something good, ya heard?" Javier nods to his big brother making eye contact only in the rearview mirror. I've never heard his brother speak. He cuts it out back there while Moises handles the money and steers with his knees. Then Javier hands up a little black baggie, like the one you get at the bodega with your forty.

"Thanks, man," I tell him. "Hey, when you gonna let me come play in that *yayo* game uptown? I'm dying to come get my *shit pushed in.*"

"Ha! In your dreams, faggot. You need anything later, sext me, bitch. I'll be out LATE to-night."

"Indeed," I tell him as we pull up to the curb. I step out and gently close the passenger-side door to his immaculate luxury automobile, as he very slowly and carefully glides into traffic.

Forty minutes later, I'm at her doorstep in East Williamsburg waiting for her to buzz me up. There's a hum and a click, and I take the elevator up with my big plastic bag full of booze, drugs, and lube. When I get up to her loft the door is open a little, and there's a sliver of warm orange light glowing out into the hallway. I push the door open, and she's standing there in this little pornographic schoolgirl outfit: the saddle shoes, the sailor's kerchief, the knee-highs, skirt rolled right up to her ass cheeks. I never asked for this. She somehow knows all of my secret perverted fantasies, and for whatever reason, goes out of her way to make them happen.

She walks up to me, that rhythmic knocking of sharp heels on wooden floors, asks me if I *have something for her*. I give her the moonrock and the blow, and she orders me to sit down on the couch. She then instructs me to eat the Viagra while she turns around toward the coffee table and bends over in my face—*the classic back-bottom-crotch-shot.* Then she starts preparing the drugs on the table's glass surface. She cuts out a few lines of the moonrock as I get to sit there and stare. I hear her snort it up her face, quick and dirty, and then she starts cutting out about ten more little lines of coke in preparation for the rest of the evening.

The thong she's wearing isn't like that regular lacey

stuff you see in the lingerie section of the Wal-Mart or wherever. Hers is some kind of heavy rolled cotton, thick like rope, like a sumo wrestler's, maybe. I guess it's some kind of *Japanese* underwear. She starts moving her ass slowly for me.

This time I really get to see all of her in the full light: the perfect pomegranate tits, the tiny toy button nipples, long thick legs. She's got a good, big, *round* ass too. Most Asian girls I'd seen had an ass like a pancake. Hers was thick, round and heavy, layered with muscle and just the right amount of fat. Thick stringy haunches flash me as she squats down and spreads. Black, wiry, natty little hairs peek out from the crotch of her panties. Then she stands up on the couch and squats down on my face.

After about 40 minutes of teasing, drinking, and some hardcore nasal activity, she turns the music way up loud and MAKES ME fuck her right there on the couch. I've got a hard-on like Valyrian steel from the little blue pill, which right now seems to count for something, as she starts coming like she hasn't had an orgasm since the towers went down. In an instant, she starts "squirting" all over my legs and her roommates' fake leather couch. I gasp with excitement, because this has never happened to me before—you know, make a woman come so hard she pisses herself (or whatever the fuck that is). I'm now soaked all the way to my knees as I dig away at her. She's screaming like she's being tortured, but she keeps pulling my ass into her harder and faster. My heart is slamming in my chest. My breathing is heavy and ragged as the sweat starts to pour. My face and head feel overheated, and I'm getting a little lightheaded. I'm pumping so hard and fast that I'm getting nervous about my vitality—the TV-commercial-warnings start replaying in my head: *ask your doctor if you're healthy enough for sex*. Faster and faster I pump away, until that old familiar burn creeps up on me. And then, just as I'm ready …

BA-BOOM!

A heavy pressure wave breaks through the apartment. The windows panes flex, and I can feel it slam through the wood in the floors. My first reaction is "Oh shit, it's the cops." But that can't be right. I'm so drunk and gacked up right now that I momentarily mistake reality for one of those god-awful sex nightmares—you know the ones—where you're in the middle of fucking an *impossible* woman and suddenly there's an epic interruption: an earthquake, a tsunami, five whipping lashing tornados catch fire right outside your window as your grandmother busts through the door in her apron and a tray of cookies while you're bare-assed and balls deep. What's perhaps more disturbing though, is that despite the obvious explosion that's just occurred right outside of her front window, neither of us has stopped— as if there's nothing more important in the world right now than me coming all over her tits. But maybe we're about to die, so maybe there isn't.

I force myself into one of those emergency ejaculations, and after I'm done she crawls out from underneath me and runs to the window, and I follow. "Oh my fuck!" she declares as we look out onto the street. The thing that caused the explosion is a silver Audi, now billowing a violent gasoline fire from its blown-out windows. Huge rolling blankets of orange and black flame violently waft and lap from all four doors. From the window, we can see what is undeniably a human figure in the driver's seat—that straight, upright torso; the left arm craned, still casually on the armrest; the perfectly round sphere of a burnt-clean human skull. She throws on her robe and me my jeans and jacket, and we run downstairs, but I'm not exactly sure why. Is it to call for help, or is it just because we're sick human beings and we really need to see this up close? Neither of us has taken our phones.

We get to the ground floor and sprint outside, and it's all right there in front of us—a human figure now almost completely charred. The flames get smaller, and there's this god-awful gasoline, burnt hair and rubber smell everywhere. There are Williamsburg kids standing all around watching like it's some kind of bonfire in suburbia. A couple of them are giggling, though I think they're too high to understand what's really going on right now. *I'm* too high to really understand what's going on right now. We're all standing there, every one of us, to some degree, high or drunk, me with a rock-hard erection still raging inside my coat. No one calls 9-1-1. No one makes any token effort to get help. None of the girls scream or cry at the sheer horror of a human being burning inside of a relatively new mid-sized luxury sport sedan. We stand there and watch someone being consumed by the flames.

12

The strangest thing as of late though, is that Harris has gone missing. Vanished, really. No calls or texts. No activity at his apartment. No social media updates or sightings at his usual titty bar. He's just *gone*—like some idiot teenager passed out wasted on a Mexican beach. The tide just rolled in and took him away. To tell you the truth, as much as I'm worried about Harris, his absence is somewhat of a relief. Lately, the man's drug problem has gotten to the point where it's been negatively affecting the lives of those around him. Harris is a glutton when it comes to H, and the signs aren't even subtle anymore: the zombie death mask; the fine spray of blood left on the wall or the toilet paper roll after he emerges from a forty-five-minute bathroom break; and the giant, weekly, opiate-compacted shit that clogs the pipes so bad that we have to call in the super with the heavy plumbing equipment. None of these things are good for business.

But then, last Monday, Harris didn't show for work. And that was the last anyone saw or heard from him.

But here we all are, still wasting our lives away in this place, like nothing ever happened. The world turns. The show goes on. A poker game still slowly squirms to life— with or without our beloved Harris.

But it has to. Somebody out there's got to make sure these people get their action. Otherwise, they're liable to burn the whole fucking city down. They're consumers. They have *demands*.

One of these assholes, yet another corporate lawyer, calls out to Matt, who's sitting at the cage. "Hey MATT! Do you guys have any WINE?"

"No," Matt tells him plainly, not looking up from his phone.

"Well, will you *send out* for some?" The guy sounds exasperated, as if he can't believe that he would actually have to ask for someone to go get him wine. Matt looks up from his phone, pauses for effect, then raises his eyebrows at the man, and tells him "No" again, before casually looking back down at his phone. Surprisingly, the guy doesn't fight him on it. He just makes a face like he's been spanked and then throws his cards at me in disgust. I casually collect them and place them gently in the muck, in a manner that doesn't at all seem like I want him to die with blood in his mouth.

One man looks over at another and notices that

they're wearing the exact same men's bracelet. Then what happens is the whole table starts talking about men's bracelets. No one's said a word for hours, and now, for some horrible reason they're all talking about jewelry. At the Taj, in AC, I once met a guy from Camden who'd been shot in the eye by a rival gang member. SHOT IN THE FUCKING EYE. Now that's worth a conversation at a poker table. Not here. Here it's Ivy Leaguers talking about lifestyle accessories and ball-busting the staff because there's no wine at the poker game. How is this still my life?

The discussion of men's bracelets then branches off into two separate asides about luxury watches and then the value of the BMW M3 versus any Porsche in the same class. The M3 wins, by the way—clearly a better value. Then it's all about Rolex. These guys *love* Rolex. "Fuck Breitling!" one of them declares. "A Breitling is NOT a Rolex. It's just not." He says this with such conviction that his voice actually cracks. Three others, also wearing Rolexes, silently nod in agreement as one guy slowly and carefully hides the face of his watch with the palm of his hand. I wonder what the boys in the industrial Midwest are talking about right now on lunch break at the cat food factory. The topics are probably so different, that to some, it must sound like a completely different language.

The men's bracelet that started this conversation is called a MIANSAI (MY-ON-SAY) which is a generic, rustic-looking sailor's hook, connected to either a thin strap of raw leather or multi-colored boat rope—both styles of which are represented at the table this evening. Turns out, one of these assholes actually knows this man who calls himself MIANSAI. He's a real guy. A real *rich* guy. Apparently, he's some kind of alpha hipster who drives around in a tricked-out Ford Bronco, but he's rich as fuck, so he's also really good at incorporating irony into his identity and lifestyle. The guy tells us that MIANSAI's family "comes from a lot of dough. LIKE, A LOT OF DOUGH," so he doesn't even need to emasculate men by selling them bracelets. He does it because "The guy just loves to *build* things, ya know?" MIANSAI also used to be a male model, so he's constantly up to his neck in pussy and he's still only in his mid-twenties. One player, out of nowhere really, suggests that he probably has a twelve-inch dick, and starts laughing out loud nervously and uncontrollably after saying so. Then another player, noticing that the dick-talker feels vulnerable, one-ups him by suggesting that *twelve inches isn't shit,* and that MIANSAI's dick must be more like eighteen inches. Then the guy who originally started talking about dicks has this horrified look on his face; he goes all pale and stops talking, as though suddenly every man on the planet has a bigger dick than he does, and now everyone knows it. Another guy chimes in by saying, "Wow, good for him, you know. Fucking

God bless him." The man who says this then pulls out a monstrous wad of cash from his pocket, wets his thumb with his mouth, peels off ten one hundred dollar bills, and wags them in the air, signaling to Matt that he needs another thousand dollars in chips, *immediately*.

Finally, Matt taps me out of the box, which means it's his turn to deal and my turn to sit at the cage and field annoying requests. "Hey TIM. Do you know where I can order *ceviche*?" Another asshole chimes in, "Yeah that sounds *amazing*. Let's order *ceviche*! Anyone else? *Ceviche*?"

"Hey TIM, can you make me a coffee?"

"Sure, how do you like it?"

"Light and *sweet*. But not TOOOO light though. I like it the color of … you know, like mocha ICE CREAM."

"Okay." I walk into the kitchen to go hide.

Suddenly there's a knock at the door. I look over at Matt who still in the box dealing the cards—the players' faces are still pointed down into their phones or up into the TV screen. No one's seemed to notice that someone's arrived, unannounced, which isn't supposed to happen in this place unless something god-awful is about to happen.

There's another knock. Louder this time. I walk over

and look into the peephole. It's the neighbor. *Fuck.* I hate the neighbor. I run into him all the time, as we emerge vulnerably from our respective units in the painful early hours of the morning—he, clearly, leaving for work, while I, clearly, am not.

He knocks again. I stand there to collect my thoughts and all of the proper faculties needed for bullshitting another man into oblivion. I look back over at Matt, who looks back at me, without expression or concern. I turn to open the door and quickly step out of the room and into the hall, shutting it swiftly, but gently, behind me.

"Hey man," I whisper, in respect for the hour. "Everything all right?"

"Listen bro, you gotta help me! My girl locked me out, and I need to get back in. I know she's just passed out wasted in there, and I've been pounding on the door for like an hour now, and I got nowhere else to go. Can I just come in and use your balcony, so I can hop over to my side and get in through the bedroom door?"

I take a deep breath, hold it in for a second, and let it out slowly, deeply, fully preparing myself to disappoint this man. "I'm sorry, buddy. I can't let you in."

Suddenly his face scrunches up in disgust, and he shrugs at me like a complete asshole. "WHY? Why the fuck not, BRO? What are you HIDING in there? I know there's some shady shit going on with you guys. I see people coming and going from your place ALL the fucking time. Like, what the fuck are you people up to?"

I look him deep in the eye. "You really want to know?" I ask him, now using a tone of serious warning.

"Yeah. What the fuck are you people DOING?"

"Well, I don't really know how to tell you this without just telling you, so I'll just say it: I host a weekly swingers party."

His eyebrows pique. I've got him.

"NO GIRLS ALLOWED," I add. "If you get my meaning …"

"Awe!" he gasps in disgust.

"And, I *don't* think that my guests would appreciate it if I just let someone walk on by while they're all naked and *sodomizing* each other. Do you? Do you think that's a good idea?"

The man is now speechless.

"And, for the record, it's none of your fucking business what I do in the privacy of my own home. Now if you don't mind, I'd like to get back to my little *get together*. Good night!"

He turns from me in silence and slowly walks off toward the elevators. I wait until he's out of sight, slip the key into the door, and go back to my living room orgy of degenerate gambling.

13

I've been feeling a little unwell these days, and it's no wonder, what with all the booze and cigarettes, the pharma-grade meth, the deli food, the non-stop Japanese pussy, the sixteen-hour workdays, and the daily gram of Ambien I need to liquefy and pump up my ass with a turkey baster just so I can fall asleep each morning. I need peace. I need convalescence. I need sensory deprivation. What I need to do is get the fuck out of New York for a while.

But right now, it's 8 a.m., and I've just gotten off work. I go back to my cheap loft in Williamsburg that I rent from a guy named Avi who I pay in cash. No one lives in this place but me. It was meant to be part of a condo development, but construction ceased right after the housing crash, so now it's essentially an Abandominium with two or three finished units and some twenty vacant, half-renovated warehouse-style lofts. Avi lets me stay here at a discount, and without a lease, since it's probably not legal to rent what's basically an abandoned work zone. Most people in their right mind wouldn't pay to live in a place like this, but I love it here. A little isolation. Plenty of room to thrash. The space is big and wooden, with stone walls, massive timbered gables, and fifteen-foot ceilings. Sometimes I feel like the king of a recently collapsed civilization, holed up in my castle with all my treasure and my larder of food, wine, and opiates—way up there all by myself, waiting to die. It's a great feeling.

On a morning like this, I like to get out the good drugs and wine, even though I have to be up in less than six hours to go do it all over again. Yeah, on a morning like this, I like to get drunk and high all by myself, turn the music way up loud, sneak off into my little walk-in closet where I hide my cash.

I turn on the light and unwrap the brown paper Duro bag where I stash it all. I add the night's pay to the pile, then I lay it all out on the bed and grab handfuls of it and squeeze it in my fists. Then I put it away and go back out into the living room and pace around some more, slam some more wine, and snort some more shit up my face. Then I walk back into my closet *again*, turn on the light *again*, take down the package *again*, count it out some more, and muse about the day I'll have enough to get the fuck out of this place. Or maybe I'll just buy something stupid like a pool table for my giant-ass apartment. *Maybe*

I'll buy a fucking used Ferrari. Yeah, just maybe, one of these days, I'll take down that package and walk right the fuck out of here. All of this money—all of this money means something. It means options—something I haven't had in a very long time.

It's approaching noon now, but since I had such a hard night and I'm feeling pretty good, I decide to treat myself to this new bag of shit I got off Moises— something he calls "crazy nigga"—a new hardcore stimulant/*possible* hallucinogen I just had to try.

So, I'm thinking, if you take enough heavy stimulants hard and fast enough, it probably has the reverse effect and acts as an anesthetic, right? You know, like the way they used to numb people out with cocaine before surgery. Yeah, that's probably how it works. So now I'm thinking, a couple hits of "crazy nigga" and a few swigs of Overholt, and I'll be out like a fucking light. Three hours of intense deep sleep and I'll be ready to get up and attack the day.

So I get good and gacked up on the shit, but about twenty minutes in, I notice that there's something a little off about this stuff. It feels like it might be half crank, half crack, or *something*. I remember hearing from a real-life crackhead at the casino one evening, that the difference between crank and crack is like the difference between driving a racecar versus driving a muscle car. I never quite figured out which was which, but whatever's going on inside me right now is indeed FAST. I get so tweaked my dick starts receding into my pelvic cavity, and I start cold-sweating while sitting there, rocking myself back and forth on the edge of my Wal-Mart futon.

I sit there just staring at my phone. *Email. Internet. Weather updates. Why? WHY?* It occurred to me recently that I am no longer a part of this thing. This *system.* I don't go out anymore. I don't go shopping. I drink alone and do drugs indoors. My banking is done inside of a brown paper bag. When the city awakens and readies itself for business, I'm trying to sleep, and while it sleeps, I'm out breaking the law and not paying taxes on my illegal income. *Life,* I've recently decided, is for other people. The joy and pain. The booms and busts. The love. The war. The responsibility. The purpose. The beliefs. The optimism. The unrelenting will to carry on with it all. It's exhausting. And yet, here I am, every day, working for a living because I don't want to die. *WHY? Why was I trying so hard?*

Panic crawls up my back and my field of vision does that Looney Tunes thing—the outside closing in towards the middle into a tiny pinhole—*That's All Folks.* I frantically stand up and walk over to the window and open it wide. I need air. I pull back the curtain and instantly the bright damning midday sun scrapes across my eyes. *SUN, NO GOOD.* I leave the window and walk back over to the bed. The low roar of the city spills into the room. I used to never notice it before, but now it's the only thing I hear—that low-fi roar—the constant grinding gears, winding everyone up and sending them into the spin of global commerce. I feel saturated by it. Steeped in the noise. That low constant rumbling, everywhere, all the time. It's hard to describe unless you've lived here for a few years. It's kind of like holding a seashell up to your ear, but instead of the ocean, you hear a bunch of assholes.

It's 3 p.m., and I'm on a humid train full of unnecessarily well-dressed people. I'm wearing a $3 black t-shirt and shoes that look as though they might serve some sort of orthopedic purpose. Across from me is a seventy-year-old man in a tweed coat pretending to read the newspaper. He's visibly uncomfortable, crammed in there with all of the younger beautiful folk, who are also not reading newspapers, but instead finger fucking their iPhones. I watch the poor old bastard as he sighs and squirms in his seat. I'm the only one who notices that he isn't actually reading. He's *hiding*—staring at the print, his eyes unmoving, turning the pages back and forth every so often so he doesn't have to look at the terrible people all around him.

And there it is, that buzz of panic again starting in my neck. Fever chills coming on, the blood draining from my face. *Train panic.* It starts in my shoulders and shoots its way up through my jaw and ears. I get tunnel vision, difficult breaths. I remember the words of Tony Soprano in the pilot episode, *like ginger ale in my skull*. Sounds amplify until it's all white noise, and my flesh feels like cold worms and wet garbage. All information is hell. There's something not right about this.

As I come off the subway onto West 4th Street, there's a twenty-five-year-old asshole in a tie, hugging a hardcover copy of *Atlas Shrugged* in the crook of his arm—like he's some kind of Capitalist Mormon or something. A true believer. Real Ivy League shit. He's standing right in front of me, somewhat blocking the exit to the subway, as he's lecturing a seventy-year-old homeless man about *the world*. "Listen, bro," he tells the old homeless man. "Only *you* can save yourself. Let me tell you about my grandfather. He was a quarter *Cherokee*." The homeless man just stares back, someplace past the kid's head, jabbering non-words into the wind. And then, perhaps unintentionally, perhaps not, the man spits right into the kid's face. The kid lets out a rather high-pitched "Oh my fucking Jesus!" and then quickly scuttles away into Starbucks to clean the venom out of his eyes. *Bathroom for customers only, motherfucker.* And suddenly, the throes of my oncoming full-blown panic attack dissolve like ocean waves over jagged dunes.

I watch the man closely, and I can see that he's completely devoid of all that makes someone a human on a conscious level, but even still, just the sight of him! The energy! His filthy bare feet; his long filthy nails; his wild, insane Don King hair; the *garment* of rags that don't even look like they were crafted in this century—all of this makes me wonder why he seems more interesting than just about every person I've ever met in the Borough of Manhattan.

As I get closer and closer to work, I walk straight past Muscle Maker Grill and dart right into the liquor store. If shit gets bad, I'm going to drink at work tonight. I don't even care anymore. As I come back out with my little black baggie clutched in my sweating palm, the bum from a few minutes before is now standing right in front of the entrance to Juice Cleanse Generation. He's screaming, "I'ma kill you, Giselle. I'ma FUCKIN KILLLLLL YOU!" There are no less than ten healthy fucks piled up at the door, waiting, *praying* for the chaos in the man's brain to cause movements in his body that will drift him away from the storefront. But he's not going anywhere, and none of these people have the balls to do anything about it. They are all trapped inside of Juice Cleanse Generation.

I smile as I watch it all and feel the bottle's reassurance of comfort in my hand.

Fuck. I'm going to be late for work.

With Harris gone a week now, Brian's been filling in until

we find a replacement for him. Brian doesn't like to work at the game, and whenever he has to be here he's a little bitch about it. It's hard to see him like this: constantly pissed off over every little detail; compulsively changing and re-changing the paper towels in the bathroom; throwing out people's drinks when they're not even finished; walking uncomfortably fast from room to room with a sense of extreme urgency, but for what, no one seems to know. It's tough working with a man who doesn't know what it is to work for a living. He doesn't know how to pace himself. He can't relax.

The KTP lately ("Korean Table Percentage") has been absolutely off the fucking chain since we moved this close to NYU. Consequently, the games have been going until the bitter filthy end almost every night—right up until the grey dawn peels through the night sky and there are three sick Korean fucks who won't leave the room until one lucky bastard gets back to even. Just thinking about another night of this shit is starting to give me the spins. Already I need some air. I've only been here for about three hours, and already I feel trapped. I decide to step out and find something to eat. I tell Brian and Matt I'll be right back. Brian looks me in the eye in this kind of eerily unfamiliar way, and then I pause and look back at him to make sure it's all right. He rolls his eyes at me and looks away in disapproval.

Whatever, man.

I walk out the door, round the corner onto McDougal and step into the first place I see. As soon as I enter, the smell of chlorine hits me hard in the nose—that hot humid chemical burn, like I've just walked into a public indoor swimming pool. I look around and I see that every dining table is set inside of a bubbling hot tub. Everyone around me is wearing a bathing suit, sitting inside of a Jacuzzi, drinking sake and eating sushi made by Mexicans dressed like Japanese artisans. I'm greeted by several tall, Caucasian, gay males dressed in kimonos and hachimaki bandannas. A particularly tall anorexic one approaches me and looks at me like, *you can't possibly want what's going on in here, dude.* In fairness, this clearly isn't the kind of place you order takeout from; the gimmick here is eating B-grade sushi inside of a hot tub. But I order it anyways because I simply don't have the gumption or energy required to go out and look for something else right now.

While I'm waiting for my absurd takeout meal, I watch a drunk white girl in fluorescent green pasties attempt to feed an overweight shirtless man a piece of sushi, as they bob around inside their VIP hot tub. The girl fumbles it, and the piece falls right into the swirling, steaming, syphilitic water. She giggles. The guy yells "Bonsai!" but no one here is offended because no one here is Japanese. I then watch this man pick up the piece of sushi out of the Jacuzzi water with his fingers, dip it into some soy sauce and pop it right into his mouth. The girl squeals with delight over his savagery, and he pulls down on her skimpy little top, flashing a couple of twenty-two-year-old perky little breasts. And for a moment, for just a split second, I wonder, very deeply, if I really have been missing out on just about everything my entire life.

I pay for my food, nervously over-tip, and blast through the exit. Heading back to the room I think about that bottle of bourbon I bought just a few hours before, and it calms me to know that all I have to do is drink it, and everything will seem just fine.

As I round the corner onto our street, I see a brand-new Mercedes Sprinter van parked right up on the sidewalk in front of our building.

Only cops are assholes enough to park on the sidewalk.

And then it hits me. The adrenals buck and pop in my blood. I get that ice-water splash of panic in the face. My stomach goes numb. I freeze. I instinctively look behind me for cops or anyone who looks like they might try and throw me into that van. But there's no one. There's no one at the building's entrance either. It's just a van parked up on the sidewalk, completely unattended. I look down at my takeout bag and throw my sushi right into a public trashcan and keep walking. As I pass the building from the other side of the street, I get a quick look inside and I can see that the second set of entrance doors have been busted wide open—little metal parts and glass all over the lobby floor.

Fuck.

I keep walking, my head looking down into my phone, my thumbs pretending to do some shit on it until I'm out of sight. Circling back around the block, I beeline it into the Chipotle directly across the street. I order a massive fountain soda and take a seat at the bar facing the window, so I can get a clear view to the front door. I text Brian and Matt something arbitrary about dinner—code for "something's up"—but there's no answer. Their phones are probably already in the sink or at the bottom of the toilet, if they were lucky enough to hear it coming.

I sit there for almost a full hour with no movement from the door. I'm not sure if I should even be this close to the building. The anticipation is tweaking me. Every jacked, clean-cut asshole who walks into the Chipotle I think is an undercover. *This is bullshit. What the fuck is taking so long?*

Finally, one by one, I see all of the bastard players exit the building, their faces pointed down into their phones, thumbs flittering, as they text their friends and girlfriends about the fucked-up shit that's just happened at the poker game—no doubt the first time they've felt alive in years.

Still no sign of police, or Matt and Brian.

I'm starting to wonder about Harris. Why he's

suddenly fallen off the grid. Not so much as a text or an email or stupid social media update. *What the fuck is going on?*

After another twenty minutes or so, I see two paramilitary-looking assholes emerge from the front door. Jarhead haircuts, black vests, cargo pants. As they step out into the daylight I can see U.S. MARSHAL tacked on their vests.

Something is very wrong with this picture. This is different from the last two raids. I don't see any Vice squad. No cruisers. No big tactical display of NYPD unnecessary force. Then, out comes another. This one dressed differently: *Good haircut.* Tall and thin. Black sunglasses. No visible weapons. *Relaxed.* He's got on khaki pants and a navy windbreaker. He steps out into the street and looks around for a bit, puts a piece of gum in his mouth, then turns his back to me, facing the building. And then I see it. Those big, fuck-off-yellow letters on the back of his windbreaker—F B I.

Before I can even process this information, I see them next—Matt and Brian emerge from the front door with another almost identical G-man escorting them gently by the shoulders—their hands cuffed behind their backs, their faces confused, mortified. This I can expect from Brian, but Matt is from fucking Russia. So, when Matt looks worried, you know it's time to *really worry*.

I check my phone for breaking news. Anything about

underground gambling, usury, racketeering charges, indictments. There's nothing.

Fucking goddamn *Wilmington*. I knew something like this would happen. Those fucking greedy cocksuckers. Always trying to pinch for a little more. Never laying off. Always moving forward with zero regard for anything but the bottom line. *Wilmington, Inc.*

I watch the Feds escort Matt and Brian into their luxury Paddy wagon, and I wait until they all clear out before I leave the Chipotle. I keep my phone in my hand, just in case Matt or Brian calls and needs me to get Josh-the-lawyer on the horn.

I keep walking, looking down into my phone in an attempt to hide the fact that I'm completely melting down in public. But just like always, no one notices. For blocks, all I see are the faces of monsters—hungry, horny, hell-bent for Friday night action. I hear foreign languages everywhere. Fake laughter. I see fashionable haircuts that look like Adolph Hitler's. Grown-ass men walking around in purple high-tops. Every three seconds a sex symbol walks by. Beautiful women. Sunglasses hide their eyes. Scarves hide their skin. I see a terrorist with a Rolex. I see a rapist with a three-legged puppy. I see illiterate models. Fitness people. Business people. Fashion people. Cool people. Tech people. *Start-up* people. Vehicle horns and ambulance sirens seem to unhinge everything. I can feel the earth washing away beneath us all ... but still ... no one notices.

When I get back to my apartment, I pack everything I need to relocate inside of a single duffle bag. I'm not leaving much behind: a discount futon, a cheap stereo, some old clothes, some toiletries, a few superficial accoutrements, and some stupid electronic gadgets that I bought whilst intoxicated. No dishes, pots, or pans. No real furniture or home entertainment system or even a real couch or a dinner table. I've never once cooked or even sat down to eat a proper meal in this place. *Fuck it. Time to go.*

I stay up all night getting rid of the rest of my drug stash—drinking, smoking, snorting it up my face, pacing around the apartment like a madman for eight hours with my shoes and coat on, my bag packed with half my cash waiting for me by the door.

Just before dawn breaks, I call Avi, my landlord, and leave a message on his voicemail. I tell him that it's all over—that I "can't get into details over the phone," but that he should know I'm not coming back. I tell him to keep my security deposit, and that I'm very sorry about the mess.

Then, as soon as the clock strikes 7 a.m.—thirty

minutes before the bank opens—I strap up and hail a cab to 42nd Street, where the other half of all my money has been stuffed haphazardly, over the last three years, into a relatively large safe deposit box.

As the sun gets fully blown, I begin coming down hard from all that expired Adderall, Oxy, and cheap emergency Overholt. It hits me fast and dirty as we come hauling ass onto FDR. Anxiety rears up on me as I clutch my bag and begin pouring sweat all over the backseat vinyl. The merciless morning sun beams down into my eyes as we barrel off the ramp. I get that awful feeling in my stomach, like I'm falling, each time the cab accelerates and rams gravity into my guts. We dip deep into the low points in the road and come swinging sideways onto the parkway. All that Sty Town concrete looms over us like Orwellian housing as we whip around the U, and then it occurs to me that that was likely the last view from the bridge I'll ever see.

I make it into the bank at exactly 7:30 a.m. I push open the doors and walk inside, but there's no one there. I get a creepy feeling, like this whole thing is a trap. *This whole fucking bank is a fucking trap.* Any second now the Feds are going to pop out and bag me—tackle my ass to the floor, cuff me and give all my cash to the IRS. Something's out of place here; like there should *definitely* be someone *in the bank* when I arrive. But I don't see anyone. No customers, no tellers, no managers, no Muzak playing. I stand there and look around for several seconds, then I hear a door click open and shut somewhere in back. A young, thin, dark-skinned island woman emerges, casually wiping her hands with a paper towel, then offers her assistance. I throw all of my shit—my duffle and one smaller backpack—right onto the polished granite floor, then nervously and somewhat frantically inform her, "I need to go to my box!" She looks at me suspiciously, which is the correct immediate reaction, then reluctantly leads me into the room. She opens the security door, glancing at me cautiously. After helping me remove my box, I ask to go into that little private masturbation room they have, the one where you're permitted to vulgarly gawk at and fondle all of your private, illegal, secret *shit*— the only place in the entire bank where there aren't any security cameras.

As soon as I'm alone, I stand there and look at it: all the money I've stashed over the last three years, balled up and stuffed there in an obvious panic. It looks so sad and so awesome at the same time. I have no idea how much is there—could be a hundred, could be two hundred thousand dollars. Frantically, I begin stuffing the loose wads of bills into a crumpled white paper Duro bag, then wrap it closed with about twenty rubber bands.

I tuck the bag of cash tight under one arm and then

call the girl in to help put back the empty box. She looks at me strangely again, as there's now one ratty white paper bag wrapped in rubber bands, half-hidden under my sweaty protective bosom. *Go ahead, honey. Report this "suspicious activity" to your masters at the IRS. I'm fuckin outta here!* I look her deep in the eye and then shrug at her like, *Hey, this is America. What the fuck do you expect?* And then I exit the bank and climb into another cab.

14

Nothing happens. For days, nothing happens. No calls. No texts from Brian or Matt, or Harris, or Josh-the-Lawyer.

I've been holed up in a Holiday Inn *Express* for over a week now. I'm not exactly sure why. For days, I've been sitting here, just *waiting*. For what, I have no idea. A call. A text. An idea. The Feds to come break down the fucking door. Anything.

So, until then, I order pizza, watch TV, and I don't leave the hotel room for anything other than beer, liquor, and cigarettes.

After about the seventh or eighth day, when I can't stand the isolation any longer, I call her. She comes over and fucks me just like she always does. She doesn't ask why I'm holed up in a Holiday Inn *Express* with pizza boxes and empty booze bottles piled up to the rafters. By now, she knows what I really am, which means she also knows better than to ask.

We fuck some more. A lot more. We go until it bleeds. Then, I finally take a shower and run out to get some more beer. I walk a little farther than I've walked since I got here. Being outside makes me feel a little saner than I've felt over the past few days. Cops walk by without seeming to know I exist. No one is outside my hotel in a surveillance van. The world doesn't seem to know or care that I'm free and that my friends are in jail. New York couldn't give two shits that I've taken well over a million dollars out of her over the past three years. I'm still a nobody. Invisible and classless. Which is a huge relief.

When I get back to the hotel room, she's kneeling on the couch in her tiny underwear, playing some kind of first-person shoot-'em-up game on PlayStation. This room did not come with a PlayStation; she brought this thing over here. She's jumping all over the couch, bare breasted, in her flossy little panties with her gaming headset on, screaming into the mic in Japanese. She doesn't bother looking over at me. Just extends her arm, making a hand gesture in the shape of a beverage—*beer me, bitch*. So I crack one open and put it in her hand, and she takes a big slurp and yells again into the headset while mashing away on the controller. Peeking out of her massive overnight bag is a Japanese-made hair dryer that looks like a giant white dildo with spikes coming off of the end of it. There is a reason, a telling of some kind, for why a Japanese lady's hair dryer looks like a massive spiked dildo, and why an American lady's hair dryer is shaped like a gun. There's probably something important there, but I don't have the energy to figure it out right now.

Anyways, I realize what I'm giving up here: a hot, alcoholic, Japanese-nympho-fuck-buddy who loves playing video games in her panties. But in light of recent events, it's become clear to me that staying in this place is suicide. I smell *serious* trouble on the way. And this time, for once in my fucking life, I've decided not to stay and wait around for worst-case scenarios. I'm leaving this place. Tonight.

After waiting patiently for her to conclude her gaming session, I ask her if she wants to stick around and watch a rerun episode of the Sopranos with me. "Free HBO," I tell her. She looks at me sadly and tells me that she has to be somewhere, then pulls up her jeans over what will likely be the best legs and ass I will ever see for the rest of my days. She puts her PlayStation and the rest of her gear back into her bag and then leaves without saying goodbye. Just like she always does. I sit there alone, as I watch the sun getting lower. I turn on the TV and open another bottle.

It's 3 a.m., and my new travel bag containing all of my worldly possessions is packed and leaning against the hotel room door: a couple pairs of cheap pants, fifteen or so black t-shirts, some new underpants and socks from the 34th Street K-Mart, a few half-drunk bottles of mid-shelf whiskey, and a white paper grocery bag stuffed to the tits with cash. This is everything I have ever owned for the past four, maybe five years.

I decide to take one last walk through the city before I leave, since I cannot picture myself having a good enough reason to ever come back here.

I step out into the night air and head southbound through Hell's Kitchen. As I pass a very familiar building, it occurs to me that I have broken the law in just about every zip code between Midtown and lower Manhattan. There really isn't an area within fifteen square blocks where I don't know a doorman, or a liquor store, or a late-night deli clerk. Every twenty minutes, I see an apartment building where I know each hallway, each backdoor exit, and the exact floor layout of every unit, because I had once been there, every night, for four to twelve months, raking money off of a felted table and skulking about the hallways in an attempt to quell suspicion among the neighbors.

As I walk on by, I feel around in my coat pocket. *Keys.*

A lot of goddamn keys. Over the years I've been collecting a great number of them. Having been removed from many a residence, I've kept spares of all the keys to all of the buildings we've occupied over the last three years. I started collecting them in case I ever found myself down-and-out again. You know, like possibly being chased by the FBI or whatever. I'd be able to sneak back into one of these buildings and find shelter in a stairwell or a covered rooftop or basement. Just for one night. Then I'd move on to another building, rotate them evenly, so no one would ever notice. *So now what?* I hold them in my hand and count them on the big ring. Fifteen. *Goddamn.* Fifteen different games. Fifteen different rooms. Fifteen absolute social nightmares. Fifteen years of my life, gone in less than five. I bounce them up and down in my hand, feeling their weight as they chime. I look over and see a public trashcan on the corner and toss them in. Maybe some insane homeless person will find them, enter a random building one evening and kill some rich piece-of-shit Wall Street cocksucker in his sleep. It's a nice thought, but I'm probably not that lucky.

Since I'm here, I decide to sneak up onto the rooftop of the old Hell's Kitchen game, one last time. I haven't been by this building in months. We were kicked out by management nearly a year ago because one of the players, drunk and unannounced one evening, knocked on the wrong door at 3 a.m. Kept knocking and knocking and pounding until some middle-aged woman finally answered her door—eyes squinting from the fluorescent-lit hallway, standing there in her nightgown behind the backdrop of a dark living room. The man then looks this middle-aged woman square in the face and tells her that he's here for the "underground poker game." These are the kinds of people who live in Manhattan.

Anyhow, I know the anatomy of this building pretty well. I know the emergency exits, the loading dock, and which stairwells lead where. I know how to get in through the *back way*, where the security camera can't see, and where I can access the north elevators through the loading dock without being noticed by Mike-the-doorman.

Once I'm on the roof, I take a drink from the little pint bottle of Vladimir I bought earlier, and I look out over the edge. The air is warm for this late in fall, and the wind feels good up here. I take another drink and stare back at the Empire State Building—*America's big ol' dick*. I look at it juxtaposed against the new glass condominium high-rises popping up all round. *What the fuck happened to this place?* No more graffiti. No more guns. No more murder or abandoned cars in the streets. No more littered newspapers blowing around in the wind. No CBGB's, or open containers, or kids sniffing glue in the parks in broad daylight. People come here to retire now—so they can see three shitty Broadway musicals a month and eat in overpriced restaurants for a few years before they die. There's nothing left to do in this town but work, drink, dine, and shop. It's a *clean* city now—one that apparently can't even tolerate a single-table poker game in the apartment of someone's living room, or a little good old-fashioned American usury. I'm done with this place. I was done with it the moment I stepped off that train.

I take one last look and spit over the side of the building, watch it fall three hundred feet down until it disappears into the glare of the streetlights. I take one more drink and make my way to the emergency exit.

As I stroll through Times Square on my way back to the hotel, it feels almost desolate—just the LED billboards brighter than the midday sun, a handful of drunk, tie-wearing asshats, a few African drug dealers, and exhausted immigrants in unlicensed Disney costumes. I see Peruvian Elmo sitting down at a table with his head off, frowning while he counts a crumpled-up pile of $1 bills. There's a new store on Broadway with a big yellow sign that reads VAPE CULTURE—SAY GOODBYE TO ANALOGUE CIGARETTES.

I really need to get the fuck out of this place.

15

I left New York that morning like a panicked yuppie in the face of a city-wide emergency Evac—bags hastily packed, passport and money stuffed in my gay little travel wallet, a rented Volvo with GPS, and a $500 emergency roadside assistance kit. The ratty white paper bag stuffed to the tits with cash that's hiding inside the wheel well is basically the only difference.

I'm headed to the *actual* "city that never sleeps." Where it's open for business twenty-four hours of every day of the year. Where the lights aren't so *inspiring*— where they coruscate with a sleazy magic, and the skyline burns with neon fire because no one gives a shit about the beach or the boardwalk anymore.

I'm driving faster than I should be, down the Expressway, glancing around my periphery for big Jersey justice hiding in the reeds. Ninety miles per hour until I hit that last tollbooth, and I can see the casino monoliths rising up out of the ocean.

I make it through the last toll unscathed, as black clouds gather over the shoreline and the vulgar casino facades instantly get bigger and brighter, beckoning to all of the world's sick and twisted idiots—people just like me.

I haven't slept in nearly thirty-six hours, but conditioning has allowed me to locate the casino garage, park nearest the elevator, and find the check-in desk almost instinctively. Before I can remember how I got here, I find myself standing in my hotel room looking out onto the midday ocean. I drop my bags and hook the "do not disturb" sign onto the outside door and immediately deposit my money into the little personal safe located inside the closet. I run the shower and crack open one of my half-drunk emergency bottles of whiskey. I haven't forgotten about the Volvo. However, the car rental agencies really should run a credit check before allowing just any shit heel with a debit card to rent a *forty-five-thousand-dollar* semi-luxury sedan. Some people in this world just don't give a fuck. Some people will just leave their responsibilities in a casino hotel garage and make your corporate asses come pick it up if you really want it back that badly. Decent credit is generally an indicator of this kind of predetermined behavior. I'm just saying.

After a nice healthy dose of mid-shelf booze and a good hot shower, I put on some socks so as not to come into direct contact with the hotel room carpeting. Then, the *complimentary* terrycloth robe.

I walk over to the window and look back out onto the ocean, the gray sky leering at me as I drink. There is indeed a storm coming. It's getting dark out there. The surf looks like rippling black tar and the low swirling clouds are thick and gunmetal gray.

It's no big secret what happens next here. My plan for the immediate future is to get good and fucked up, and then sleep for I don't know how long. And when I awaken, I'm going to have no less than three cups of coffee and a lavish meal, and then I am going to go down onto that casino floor and I'm going to gamble, all by myself, for a very, *very* long time.

I take another drink from the bottle, and I walk over to the bedside and sit down in my robe and socks and turn on the television. Three talking heads are all lined up there on the news channel, yelling over one another about some damned thing. I sit there and stare, retaining none of it, as my mind drifts away from me. I glare into the glowing screen, breathing slowly. Minutes go by, maybe longer. I feel the bottle in my hand again and take another drink and look over on the nightstand. Room service. *Shit.* I grab the menu, open it up, and before me is a page entitled "Comfort Classics," in eloquent, embossed cursive lettering. On the very top of the page is an item called a "Chicken Bacon Deluxe," which is described to me as "an eight ounce flame broiled breast, adorned with thick-cut savory bacon, caramelized onions, melted Swiss cheese and smothered in our chef's signature Ranch Dipping Sauce." Seventeen dollars plus an eighteen-percent, in-room dining gratuity. I look back up at the television for a second while considering this, and I think to myself ...

That actually sounds pretty fucking good.

ABOUT THE AUTHOR: Very little is officially known about John Curry, other than that he lives somewhere on the Isle of Manhattan and is intimately familiar with the world of underground poker in New York.

Love the book? Hate the Book? Tweet at John about it. John loves criticism and people who go out of their way to publicly criticize shit all over the internet. He believes they're important to our culture. @curry_writer.

77499710R00097